NOBODY'S SUPPOSED TO BE HERE

NOBODY'S SUPPOSED TO BE HERE

THE STORY OF MY OBSESSION WITH A DARK BORDERLINE

Claude Joseph

To order additional copies of this book, contact:
Xlibris
844-714-8691
www.Xlibris.com
Orders@Xlibris.com
827286

Table of Contents

ACKNOWLEDGMENTS

I would like to sincerely thank these wonderful people for their contribution to my first book. Their expertise was astounding, from the book model, editors, supportive friends, advisors to the people I consulted.

Cover Model-Nyashaa Najee Waheed

Who Inspired the Book Title-Ruthalee Brundidge/ Deborah Cox (R&B Singer)

Developmental Editor-Jennifer Kizzee

Cover Designer-Robert Bowman

Publishing Company-Xlibris Publishing Company

Also, I would like to thank La Shaun Cay, Charles Beasley, Kevin Anderson, Henry Westerfield, Shalonda Lee, Stewart Thomas, Pintoya Beauman, Raymond Porter and Niocha Hishaw for their unconditional support. It was over this 6-year run, I thought I would never complete this book, but I never gave up. But it was these great friends who believed in me and motivated me to keep going.

Thank You.

SYNOPSIS

Ask yourself this question?

If good girls like the bad boys, then who do the nice guys like? Of course, the science is not definitive, but the answer may lie within this story…..

This is a tale of a millionaire in New Orleans who seems to have it all, but what you don't know is that he has a fatal flaw; he's attracted to the wrong women. The ones that smell like trouble from a mile away, and this one in particular had her demons on her shoulders. She wore them like a badge of honor. She has a Borderline Personality Disorder, pulling several weights of troubling history, and evil agendas. Her name is Andrea Locket, the alluring beauty who poses as a dainty maid for hire to get what and who she wants. Eliminating anyone who stands in her way.

But why would a man fall for a woman with so much baggage? Why didn't he just run the other way?

I'm glad you asked because I know you are curious about the reason why. But nothing is just black and white, there is always some grey. There's usually much more to things than we can see. That is why you must take this journey with me to where it all began.

The man in is story is me, Lonnie Guy, who invites you to take a ride with me on this erotic, wild journey of how she became who she is; and why I stayed.

INTRODUCTION

To every story, there is always a backstory. Wheels are always turning behind the scenes, steering the motion we see. And in this tale, we will start with those wheels.

A look at the situation before she even stepped into the ring. This is going to be storytelling that you will understand. It is not an excuse, but a version of the narrative from the eyes of a broken woman who never stood a chance.

'Nobody's Supposed to Be Here' is inspired by a woman with Borderline Personality Disorder. As this tale progresses, you will meet everyone who played a part in her journey because every person has a story to tell.

This entire book recalls a hit song from the 1998 hit song by Deborah Cox.

I've spent all my life

On a search to find

The love who'll stay for eternity

The heaven-sent to fulfill my needs

But when I turned around

Again love has knocked me down...

Nobody's supposed to be here

But you came along and changed my mind...

Like my book, the song centers around a woman whose life has been damaged by broken love, a neglectful childhood, and the men who were there for her through her struggles.

And in this tale your about to read, you will get a front-row seat to how everything starts to unravel. There are no heroes in this tale. Just people whose paths cross and they manage to influence each other in ways that are not simple.

Her name is Andrea Locket.

The woman whose story I'm telling. She had a rough childhood, and you will know the details of that soon. Her version of the narrative shows how she was a victim of her environment and how she reacted to the situation around her. Then the narrative moves to when she starts to take charge of her life when she meets a security guard named Terrance Black at a poorly run hotel in which they work.

Together they devised a plan to manipulate wealthy men out of money and gifts using her arresting looks. The plan was initially meant to benefit both partners, but unfortunately, things went wrong, and the authorities got involved. Due to the fear of getting caught, they had to go on the run, shedding their old lives and changing their identities.

Now on her new suspenseful journey as Simone, her new name, she sets her sights on a bigger target; his name is Lonnie Guy. A rich, good looking nice guy that cannot resist the lust he has for her. Coincidentally, his desire grows into a conscious love and an unconscious obsession.

But as she gets closer and closer to the fairy-tale love she craves; she is confronted by many bad elements that awaken her Borderline past darkness. There was no way to hide her demons from him. If only he could save her from herself but remember, "He wasn't supposed to be there."

CHAPTER ONE

CRACKING THE CODE

It was a cool evening, one of the last days of spring; picturesque from where I'm sitting. Alone on one of the park benches watching people enjoy a casual walk, taking in the quiet, and soaking the magic of tranquility.

I quirk my lips in a half-smile when I spot an elderly couple approaching me hand in hand. It seemed like they were hanging on to each other for dear life but in a sweet way. It was probably the synchronization.

They walked together, one leg in front of the other, in harmony, a demonstration of love that only time can foster. For a split second, I let myself imagine that that could be her and me.

A dry chuckle escapes when I think of how ridiculous it is to even think of this with our complicated situation. I shake it off with a sigh. These moments are coming too few and far between, because my eagerness is beginning to get the best of me. It's been three whole weeks since our last sexual encounter, and ever since then, it has been on my mind.

The last time was mind-blowing. I have re-lived every single second of it over and over in my head for the past week. And for a long time, I thought it was the sex—which is incredible, but there is so much more to her. Her smell, those mesmerizing eyes, her soft skin, her husky voice drifting in and out of my life, was driving me insane.

It was on a Saturday night right here at our favorite park in Metairie, Louisiana. I had checked the time on the watch; it was 11:20 pm, which was just 40 minutes before the park closed to the public. It appeared that we were the only two left, which was cool except for the security guard patrolling.

We waited patiently and undetected until we knew he was gone. Once we knew he was gone, all bets were off; we started making out on our favorite park bench.

The weather was perfect; it set the scene. The temperature was 74 degrees and clear. Perfect for romance and some heavily sensual lovemaking. I could feel it in the air, the electric cackle we emit whenever we are together, and she could feel it too, even more than I did.

At this point, she took control of our make-out session, and her rare spontaneous side kicked in. Visualize me sitting on the left side of her on the park bench and her aggressively forcing my right hand down the front of her panties.

Her breath was warm on my neck as her teeth gave me a little bite. All my inhibitions flew out of the window when she whispered in vivid detail, explaining what she was feeling and what she wanted me to do in her husky tone.

If you combine all the elements of that evening, the mood, the scenery, the danger of doing what we were doing in such a public place, and her tongue finding its way deeper into my mouth— there was no way I could easily forget a night like this.

She wore a two-strap white summer floral dress and a musky fragrance that seems to be the perfect blend of everything I love. At this point, my libido is at an all-time high, and I am ready to be taken over the edge. As she continued to do what she was doing with her hand, things got even hotter.

Dominance was the word that popped up in my mind. She removed her dress right there in the park while I sit in awe. Shocked and excited would probably be the best way to describe my emotions at that moment. She continued her wild movements by placing my hands on her breast while moaning out of control.

I used to feel intimidated by all her aggression, but it was time I stepped up to the challenge and became the guy she was craving. I grabbed her arm, spun her around, pushed her head forward, and began kissing and licking the sweat off her back down to her butt.

I am now volcanically aroused; I penetrated her from the back with my penis, causing her to orgasm within minutes, and then she blacked out. It seemed as if she was in a deep mania of energy, and within a split second, it was over almost as quickly as it started.

Immediately her memory came back; the first thing that came out of her mouth was, "What did you do to me?" She flipped the script big time. This was not the first time she pulled this kind of crap on me. It took me a while to put it together, but there is a routine to it—the spontaneity, then the mania, then the lashing out, and then the regret.

The regret usually happens the next day or the same night. She would say things like, "This is the last time I will ever have sex with you outside." I knew what she was saying was bullshit, but as always, I nodded my head yes in agreement and looked forward to the next episode. I'm assuming this is where my obsession originated-the thirst for more and more. After catching the brunt of this behavior for so long, it started to wear on me mentally and emotionally.

Perhaps this incident led me to research her behavior. I did not know what I was looking for per se; but I was sure her behavior was not normal. After a proper glimpse of her dark side and research, I detected she had Borderline Personality Disorder.

I thought she was acting out for the most part, but there were layers to her behavior that kept me puzzled most of the time. Once I determined what she had, then the other layer began to surface. There were rumors of her being sexually promiscuous, a killer, and a manipulator.

My naive and glass-half-full attitude would never let me welcome such a notion is true, but I could not help it; there was no point ignoring the signs. In my mind, I held on to the belief that there was no way she would be capable of anything like that, or was she?

Again, call me obsessed, but at this point, I did not care. I just had to know, so I put on my psychologist hat and began to embark on a tremendous journey for the truth. I just had to dig deeper. There had to be a bigger story. Some depth that was impossible to recognize when seen at just face value. I needed to know how she became this way, but the answers I sought were in her past.

Fortunately for me, I got a breakthrough. Well, more like I got lucky because there were no other means, I could not have found out about her past anywhere else. Who else could have told the story better than herself? When I stumbled upon a plethora of information she had stashed, I was shocked. It was several rough drafts and notes she put together in hopes to one day write a biography.

They were detailed accounts of her existence. I guess she just felt the need to document everything to make life feel real.

For a long time, I knew all the answers I needed were in those manuscripts. My glimpse into the mystery that surrounded her was so close, but I could not bring myself to look through them. Then a day came when everything came crashing, and all my inhibitions flew out of the window. There was an incident that led her to become unresponsive.

Against my better judgment, while she was recovering from a traumatic injury, I opened a box marked "my life" and started reading. I just had to know more about her. The box included a lot of detailed information such as investigative reports, psych evaluations, newspaper clippings, different addresses, multiple IDs, and a diary she later used to keep up with her daily interactions if she ever blacked out again. The diary was a mystery within itself because she kept the key to it as a charm on her gold necklace.

Therefore, with all these resources at my disposal along with my accounts of what happened; I can tell her story, and here it goes.

Let's start from the beginning...

Her name was Andrea Locket; she was born to a gangster family. Her father —Monroe Locket— had the good sense to invest some of his drug money in a hotel that he ran with his partner, Smitty.

These two men had been childhood friends and partners in crime. Andrea's mother, Rae, came into the picture as an immigrant sent by her parents from the Dominican Republic. And even though she had no education or prospects in the United States, she hoped her looks would score her some luck, and she would catch the eye of a man who would marry and take care of her.

Rae worked in the same hotel that Monroe and Smitty owned but in the sales department. When Rae's beauty started to become talked about around town, even Monroe could not help himself. Soon, he started finding different reasons to spend time with Rae even though he was oblivious to his partner.

Smitty was attracted to her too and was hoping that Monroe, since he had the looks, would recruit her to be their trollop or pass around;

he ignorantly thought he could also get a turn. Still, after working closely together, Rae and Monroe became close. So close till they started dating. Rae Johnson was once the most admired young lady in the neighborhood. She had the kind of beauty and spirit that most women envied. Monroe, on the other hand, was not your ideal mate.

Yes, he was a handsome, witty, street-savvy black man, but he also stayed in trouble and was feared by his peers. The only time he ever smiled was when he was in the presence of Rae. They were crazy about each other.

They tried keeping their romance a secret from Smitty because Monroe did not want anyone to find out that he was falling for Rae, especially since he had many enemies. But an enemy he did not count on was the one right under his nose. Even though Smitty met her first and gave her the job, she was not interested in him.

Smitty was mean, cocky, and out of shape. Smitty liked to prance around wearing his expensive clothes and jewelry while barking unnecessary orders to the employees. He was unbearable to deal with, especially to the women. No one liked him, especially not Rae.

After some months, Rae discovered she was pregnant with Monroe's child; there was no use hiding it anymore. It was Monroe's child, and they agreed to name her Andrea.

They officially announced their relationship, got married, and took their chance at whichever version of happily ever after was in the stars for them. Monroe and Rae loved each other, and he did everything he could to protect his little family.

Andrea was born a few months after their union; she was the perfect adorable baby everyone loved to describe. Her mother finally got what she wanted; a beautiful family and a man that could provide for her. They were happy. What could ever go wrong? If only they knew what fate had in store for them.

They lived in their quintessential bubble for sixteen years. Monroe tried to go legit, but Smitty was adamant that Monroe keeps his street persona for just a bit longer until they get the proper security. Smitty knew that if the respect were lost, their enemies would try to destroy them and the hotel.

Monroe continued to be a model father and husband, but this did not stop him from being a criminal. Monroe was careful; he always played his cards right. If there were anything like honor among thieves for gangsters, then this circumstance was definitely equal to that saying.

When new evidence surfaced that eventually led to Monroe's arrest, it surprised everyone. It had to be someone very close to him that gave him up, but no one could prove it.

He got arrested by the police. He had been under investigation for multiple assault charges for years. The evidence that surfaced was enough to indict. After a lengthy trial, he was found guilty and sentenced to 50 years in prison. But before he got processed in, he left his 24-carat gold necklace he never took off to Andrea and made everyone in their circle swear never to touch it.

Monroe going to prison affected both Andrea and Rae but in different ways. Andrea had to pick up the abandoned pieces of a once happy family. Simultaneously, Rae was left to deal with Monroe's lawyers' legal fees while also figuring out their financial survival.

It got worse when Monroe's assets were all seized by the government, except for the hotel. Monroe did not add his name on the hotel ownership intentionally because of the possibility of the Feds taking it.

He knew that if he ever got busted, the Feds would think he bought the hotel with illegal money. Instead, Smitty's name was listed as the owner of the Airport Hotel. Monroe has an equal stake in the hotel as well, although not on paper.

As you can imagine, with Monroe out of the way, Smitty could do what he wanted with the hotel and Rae. Despite the rumors, Smitty was the one who allegedly masterminded Monroe's arrest, but no one could prove it. For instance, the hotel staffers often saw what looked like detectives whispering to him. It just seemed fishy. Once Monroe got arrested, they wanted to know why didn't Smitty go down too. Hmmmm….

Who knows? But in the meantime, Smitty took advantage of both opportunities. First, he changed the name from the Airport Hotel to Smitty's Extended Stay Hotel. A simple move to stamp his foot on the hotel when Rae started making claims about her husband's stake in the business. He told her that the hotel belonged solely to him now, but he was a terrible businessman.

The hotel was located just six miles from the Detroit Metropolitan Airport. It was a gold mine for making money because of its prime location and beautiful décor Monroe made sure of, but none of that mattered to Smitty. He only cared about the bottom line. The hotel's problems started because Smitty was a slum lord whose cheapness made him lose a lot of business.

Due to his incompetence, the hotel had a mice infestation, roaches, and poor maintenance. But he did not care as long as he was making money, and Monroe was out of the picture. He finally had his opportunity with Rae, and he knew he had her at a disadvantage.

Rae tried to stay committed to Monroe through all of this debacle, but her efforts were in vain. The sales job just was not enough to keep things afloat. She was back to square one; they lost their house, their cars, her husband and was left with high bills, and debt. Due to this adverse effect, she was desperate, and Smitty knew this. So, he bids his time before he makes his proposal to Rae. He would let her stay rent-free for an extended stay at the hotel, but she had to fulfill his sexual needs.

Rae tried desperately not to take the deal, but she had no choice. She was getting harassed by the people she owed money to, and even her daughter was not safe in the neighborhood they lived.

She knew she had no other option, not in a country where she is undocumented and uneducated. But for the sake of her family, she made one last plea and begged Smitty not to let her compromise her morals, having to cheat on her husband. But Smitty did not care; her request went in one ear and right out the other.

Eventually, Rae accepted the proposal and went from being a good wife and mother to something more sinister. In addition to the sexual favors, she had to comply with, she could only keep a small part of her sales job salary which was next to nothing. She was always on call, and to top it all off, Smitty was in complete control of her life.

CHAPTER TWO

SPIRALING DOWN

Following Monroe's arrest and trial, Rae did all she could, but all her efforts were futile. The lawyers kept lying and leading her on by promising to help Monroe, but they were just extorting her and Monroe for more money in all actuality. They pressured Rae to take out shady loans that they knew she couldn't pay back to secure Monroe's ridiculous retainer fees.

Monroe assumed he would get out soon, and when he did, he would be able to clear the debt from people who owed him money. However, he never made it out. Instead, things got worse for Rae as she had to sell almost all their possessions that the government had not taken away.

Her lack of resources also took its toll on her daughter, Andrea, whose life changed too. Not only could she not afford what she was used to, but they also had to sink into a new low. For a teenager, she had no way of knowing the magnitude of hell that was yet to come.

At first, Rae visited Monroe in prison with her daughter, but she soon stopped when she started to give herself to Smitty. Her not coming piqued his curiosity as he looked to Andrea for answers. Since Andrea continued her visits, he thought she would brief him on what was going on, but she didn't. Instead, Andrea remained neutral despite Monroe's consistent efforts. It's safe to say she did not want to be in the middle of Rae and her father's drama.

It was no surprise when Rae got depressed. And to cope with her depression, she turned to recreational drugs. Drugs played a role in her spiraling down to the point that both Andrea and Smitty were affected. Andrea got it the worse because Rae started taking things out on her.

She became a terrible person who did not even remember she had a teenage daughter to raise. Smitty grew tired of Rae being a frail addict and reneged on the deal. When Smitty gave Rae a job and a place to stay, the other stipulation was to sleep with him, but with her being an addict, Smitty could now kick Rae and Andrea out. To keep her job, which was a way to continue to get drugs and secure their place to stay; she agreed to give her daughter to Smitty when he threatened to cut her off.

As soon as Andrea turned 17 and legal, she got exposed to sex for the first time. Her mother sent her to Smitty, and he just stood there while pleasuring himself, staring at Andrea's naked body without even touching her. She wanted to laugh, but she continued to hold it in just long enough until he was done.

Smitty doing that was weird to her, but at the same time, it was the first time she ever saw a man naked up close, and she liked it. That incident changed her life in minutes, thrusting her into adulthood. From that point on, with the use of some potent marijuana, it got a lot easier when she had to fuck Smitty and his friends. She will probably never admit or even identify that this was her version of her hoe phase, more noticeably to her in her interactions with boys at her school. She had a secret desire to become sexually promiscuous, a volcano of lust ready to get out, but she knew she could not act on it, because there would be terrible social consequences between her and her peers.

When the guys approached her, she shunned them away. Andrea would not even look them in the face. She just kept her head down and ignored them, not because she wasn't interested or sexually attracted to them but specifically because she didn't want what was going on at home to come out. No one knew in-depth how bad it was for her at home, but no one also knew how twisted the darkness of her mind was getting.

The same with the girls at school, but differently, she was embarrassed because she could not afford what the other girls had, such as the bare necessities like toiletries or decent clothes. Andrea was pretty, but she saw how the popular kids treated the poor kids, which made her feel socially incompatible.

Fortunately for Andrea in school, the teachers were very partial to her because of her living conditions. She wasn't getting the love and nourishment she needed, so the staff often stepped in.

They did little things to help, like sneak her money and snacks. They made life a little easier for her. One Friday evening, one of her high school teachers, Ms. Sheila, decided to throw out some old movies.

She specifically asked Andrea if she wanted any of them. Andrea replied, "Yes, I do." Ms. Sheila gathered them up and handed them to her. As she gathered them up, Ms. Sheila pointed out the one called The Stepfather and said, "This one requires you to be at least 18 years old or older to view."

Andrea replied, "It's okay. I watch graphic material all of the time." Against Ms. Sheila's better judgment, she gave all the movies to her, including The Stepfather.

The teacher was right; the movie did affect Andrea in ways she couldn't have ever imagined. The movie The Stepfather is about a man who appears to be the ultimate nice guy, a gentleman, but his niceness is deceiving. He moves from place to place, changing his identity and charming single-mothers into love and a stable home.

But when his pretty picture wasn't so cute, and his real identity gets exposed. He would kill his accusers and move on to the next city, leaving no evidence behind. It was Andrea's favorite movie, and she watched it over and over.

To her, the movie was an outlet, a quick mental getaway that was crucial in the first place. Watching a man get away from his exploits and the thrill he got was invigorating to her. To Andrea, that showed a man that oversaw people's fate.

He did not need permission from anyone to indulge in his wildest fantasies. This notion gave room for a deep pondering of the dark while pretending to be a normal American teenage girl.

As for Rae, she took the opposite route. She continued to use recreational drugs, which made her body start to deteriorate. She grew very frail and thin. Her skin went pale, and she became uninterested in everything that did not involve getting high. She did not even care about her daughter or anybody else for that matter.

But Smitty did care, he had plans for Andrea, and it was time to solidify the deal to take Andrea off Rae's hands for a fee. But before the ink was dry and the deal was signed, he had to know for sure that Andrea would know her place or at least know she was at a disadvantage. But who in their right mind would stand by and let the rug get yanked right from under them with no push back? Not Andrea. Of course, she couldn't do much about Smitty because he had all the leverage, but as far as her mother Rae was concerned, she was fair game. She left it up to karma and fate to take care of Smitty.

It was time to cut Rae loose. He offered Rae ten thousand dollars for Andrea's rights, which would include her going away and staying out of the way for good. It would be an adoption agreement on paper, but truthfully, it was slavery for Andrea and free labor for him.

Smitty could not risk Rae getting clean and trying to save her daughter. He took pleasure in knowing that Andrea was under his control while he and his friends continue to take advantage of her as long as they could. It was no surprise when her mother, Rae, took the deal Smitty offered her and began preparing to leave to go back to the Dominican Republic.

She felt like there was nothing in America for her anymore. Monroe was going to be in jail for a long time, and she had become a shadow of herself. When Smitty offered her the payout to leave, she did not think twice about taking the chance to return home; there was just only one loose end for her. She had to tell Andrea, and she was not stupid.

She was avoiding telling Andrea the truth of why she was leaving or that Smitty is paying her. Instead, she started to paint the future of new expectations and the new reality for Andrea. She told Andrea, "I will be going away soon, and you'll be fine here with Smitty.

You'll be eighteen soon, and then you can come to join me. But you are American, and you belong here. I must return home to get my life together; I can then take better care of you. There is no one else here apart from Smitty to care for you. I am sorry I am going to leave you with him; I have no other option.

You cannot come with me now. Just hold on. I know you will survive. You are a smart, beautiful young lady. I trust you can take care of yourself. Plus, I am only going to get better.

The adoption is for legality so that the state will not take you away. Don't worry, ok? I will always be your mother; I have to leave for a little while."

At least that's what she told Andrea, but really, she wouldn't dare to tell Andrea everything that transpired between her and Smitty. As you can expect, Andrea did not take this news well. Even though her mother was being selfish, she took solace that Rae was the only family she could lean on.

If Rae left now, not only will she be left at the mercy of Smitty, but she would also be all alone. Especially since Monroe stopped accepting visitors from her and Rae, there was literally nowhere else to turn.

He told Rae and Andrea never to come and see him again the second month after his sentence. Prisoners from their last visit were luring at them, and two of those prisoners were about to be released. Monroe feared these guys may try to go after his family to get to him since he was now considered a badass in prison and holds the keys. He wanted them to think his family had abandoned him. Therefore, for their sake, he did what he had to do.

Andrea tried to visit a few more times, but every time the guards turned her away. This was why her mother's wanting to leave affected her even more. She threw a fit and did not accept her mother's explanation. She was scared and did not let her mother off the hook with her flimsy excuse.

She took her mother's passport and hid it in a place where she could never find it, which was in her cleavage. She wanted answers, and when her mother confronted her about the passport, she yelled at her mother, "you'll get it back when you give me some answers." I'm not stupid; your bags are all packed.

You do not intend to come back, Mom! Is that your plan; to leave your daughter with a gross pervert? I cannot believe you, Mom.

Rae tried to explain, "What I'm doing is what's best for you." But really, she was only doing what was best for herself. Smitty got tired of the bickering back and forth, so he intervened and ended the dispute by saying, "Both of you be quiet." Andrea give her back her passport. Andrea grudgingly handed it back over. Smitty then said, "Rae can come back once she gets sober." Andrea didn't have much faith in what Smitty was saying because Rae was in bad shape, and Andrea had a good idea of what was to come for herself.

Smitty took Rae to the airport, and Andrea rode with them. Once they were there, Andrea begged Rae to take her with her. She said, "Momma, you can't leave me here!" Rae replied, "I'm sorry I can't take you. I have to do this for myself; you'll be fine here."

Andrea looked Rae in the eye in disgust and blanked her eyes before she spoke in a chilly low tone and said, "I hope you burn in hell, and for now on, you are no longer my mother." Rae did her best to avoid the guilt she felt, so she just continued boarding the plane as planned. And in the blink of an eye, she was gone.

Andrea was left to pick up the pieces in a state of confusion and numbness. The question was, 'So, what now?' She asked herself after hours of staring at a wall. She did not cry. No. She just kept a straight face and continued to ask herself whether the universe would provide an answer and give her direction of what she would do with her life.

But she knew one thing for sure; she would not break like her mother. She knew she had to persevere. She had no choice. She already had hit rock bottom.

Andrea promised herself that she would do anything to better the odds despite how the coming years get hard. No matter what it takes. She decided to assess her situation and take note of what she had logically. She took a mental inventory of her assets, good looks, and the ability to manipulate men. For the longest time, she had covertly been exploiting Smitty, so she was somewhat ready for the lifestyle.

She used to do it for the minor things, like getting out of chores and making sure he gave her some loose change. Andrea was the offspring of an attractive-looking interracial couple, which proved immensely beneficial in her quest to survive. Rae was from the Dominican Republic, and Monroe was an African American from Chicago.

She had good genes that served her well, what some people described as an Exotic look. She was gorgeous and had a remarkable body. High rise round breasts with perky nipples helped her get away with not wearing a bra half of the time. She had a tiny waist, a luscious ass, and a perfect figure.

Andrea took stock of what she had and used her attributes to get what she wanted. She did not see herself as a victim anymore; the men she came across while underage became her victims. Most of them were still around; that's why she kept video-proof hidden away in her cell phone just in case she ever needed it. And now was the time. Although it was no sex or assault involved, the men thought they could get away with soliciting a minor. But they were so wrong because they had to pay Andrea off with lots of hush money. Even Smitty became afraid of her, and when he got his cancer diagnosis, he became too weak to want her.

CHAPTER THREE

THE HUSTLE BEGINS

After flunking out of high school her senior year, Andrea went to summer school and finally graduated; it was apparent that she did not want to further her education and go to college. Andrea struggled to get through school and did not care about what she learned in the classroom. She just wanted to make money and not be poor or helpless like her mother.

She continued working in the hotel without having to deal with Smitty's manipulations. He eventually left her alone and concentrated on his health and business.

Andrea was doing her daily housekeeping duties at the hotel, some male guests often suggested sex. The male guests were willing to pay her for it, and she needed the money.

At first, she was scared that she would finally have to sell her body, but she got help. And that help came from a new friend and acquaintance she made at the hotel. His name was, Terrence Black and from the first day he stepped into the hotel lobby, Andrea knew that they would be connected. It was not even sexual at first. It was something about him that drew her to him.

He had an aura of struggle and strength aced with the right amount of edginess and darkness. Terrence must have felt this too; he was confident and attractive with his movie-star looks, charming smile, and all the other girls wanted to be with him, but he befriended Andrea.

Soon they started talking, and they talked about everything—their past, family, and ambitions. One thing was for sure; these two ambitious souls had the same zeal to make sure they do not end up poor since they did deserve better. Therefore, they promised each other that they would do everything and use everything at their disposal to make themselves better.

Everyone called him "Black," and by being older and wiser, he knew or heard of several different schemes from the past that they could one day do to get rich. At first, they laughed it off, but they both knew that they were open to new hustles that could profit them in the long run, illegal or not.

With this newfound courage from Black, Andrea was open to new and better ways to hustle. So, they moved forward with the planning; Black took on Andrea as his protégé to show her the correct way to make her money.

Black noticed the earning potential right away and recruited two other housekeepers, Serenity and Carissa, to solidify his plan. He found a way to help these ladies get with the right men who came in as guests into the hotel and make money.

It was an organized prostitution scheme. Serenity was the quiet one and the sidekick to Carissa. Carissa had a robust, aggressive personality, and she challenges you when she feels something wrong is happening.

Once Black got all his recruits, he called a secret meeting in one of the conference rooms to direct them on what and what not to do. Smitty was out of town most of the time, so all Black had to do was keep up with his arrival and departure dates. And since Black was usually the one that dropped Smitty off and picked him up from the airport, he was able to stay two steps ahead.

The hustle was good and lucrative for a year. Then things began to go awry when one of the other housekeepers noticed a paranoia pattern in Andrea's behavior. The paranoia mostly took place during the times Andrea smoked marijuana.

The first incident was when Andrea and Serenity were assigned to a room to clean together by the front desk. While cleaning the room, Andrea saw a reflection in the mirror that frightened her. She told Serenity that the reflection in the mirror was The Stepfather.

Serenity replied, "Who the hell is The StepFather?" Andrea quickly came around and took stock of her surroundings, gathered herself, and responded to Serenity, saying, "Never mind, I'm tripping." But then it got worse.

Andrea started getting sloppy and reckless when having sex with the guest. She would sometimes sleep with strangers without the use of protection. She was constantly risking the chance of getting pregnant and getting an STI or STD. It wasn't a month that didn't go by that she didn't have a Plan B morning-after crisis.

Carissa was one of the first to observe Andrea's erratic behavior. There was an incident one day that brought attention to Andrea's situation. Black had assigned Andrea and Carissa to a hustle job to meet up with some guys in one of the hotel rooms.

The next day Andrea told Carissa her ass hurts, and she was anal raped. Carissa replied, "No, you were not. I was there in the other bed beside you the whole time." Carissa had retorted in a challenge about Andrea's accusation.

She went on to clarify and reminded Andrea of what happened in the room the previous day. "They requested two girls; don't you remember? We smoked, and you repeatedly insisted on trying anal for the first time. You even said you were enjoying it and kept going for an hour. Then you started acting strange and then passed out.

You were rubbing the outside of your right hand diligently while looking off in space and asking weird questions like 'What if we are aliens?' Carissa stared at Andrea as she still tried to feign ignorance; Carissa knew for sure she had remembered what happened the previous night.

She got a glimpse of what Andrea was capable of when she accused those guys of rape. But she acted like that because Andrea hates gray areas when she blacked out and didn't know what happened. She automatically thought the worst and believed everyone was out to hurt and take advantage of her.

It was only a matter of time; the string of unusual and erratic events became known to the girls around the hotel. The pattern of chaos is associated with Andrea that needed to be brought to Black's attention.

When the girls got the courage, the hotel guests informed them that Black and Andrea were messing around in secret and were beginning to have feelings for each other.

If what was said by the guest to be correct, that would mean Black, and Andrea would be in direct violation of their initial arrangement. The agreement stated that Black could not get involved with any of the girls romantically. Those lines could not be crossed, and there would be no favoritism when Black assigned jobs.

When confronted, Black denied having any romantic involvement with Andrea and began to lash out at the two girls, Carissa and Serenity. He got defensive when he heard the girls talking about not wanting to work with her anymore.

They wanted her out of the group. They felt like she seemed dangerous and posed a threat to the rest of the girls and even the customers. But Black just dismissed their allegations against Andrea and said, "You're hating. She can't be that bad."

Carissa responded with an assertion that should have been a sign of how serious the situation was. She looked into Black's eyes and said, "Open your eyes, dude, you're tripping, but you'll soon see. You're so damn naive, Black! Get your head out of the clouds before it's too late." I have no time for this," Black retorted and stormed off, telling the girls to get back to their world.

They weren't feeling Andrea at this point, but likewise, she wasn't feeling them either. Andrea was fully aware and could sense the negative energy surrounding her. She knew the girls could barely stand her at this point and wanted her out of the business. They even went out of their way to avoid and never agree to have threesomes that involved Andrea.

Nevertheless, it started to get to Andrea when she saw the girls snickering behind her back and following her around, trying to catch her in the act of doing something shady so they can have proof. Instead of retaliating, initially, Andrea selected to take the high road. Eventually, she could not hold back the dark borderline characteristics which are continuing to brew within her.

She pulled Black aside one day and told him about the girls. Black had to protect the business, and since the girls were already suspicious, he expressed to Andrea to just let it go. Andrea knew he did not intend to do anything; She just slowly spread her lips in a smile that did not reach her eyes. She reached out and patted Black's cheek and said, "If you don't handle them, then I will."

Black received the message loud and clear. Even he was scared that the situation had escalated and was not sure of what Andrea can or will do. He got the news of her casual threat clear and knew he could not ignore it any longer.

He listened to everyone's concerns and placed the hustle on hold until he figured things out since the organization was crumbling right before his eyes.

The girls' relationship kept getting worse, and the only bright side was that Smitty wasn't due back in town until the beginning of the year. Andrea knew that; hence, she solicited Black to take her away from this run-down hotel and this life.

She wanted to go somewhere, anywhere far, far away. Andrea's motivation to move quickly resonated with Black; luckily for her, his naiveté was at an all-time high. He was blinded so much by Andrea's body and good looks until he ignored her mental state and proceeded to plan a getaway.

The plan was to leave a day or two after Christmas, just a few weeks after the suspension of the hustle. As time grew near, Black and Andrea had to be very careful and low-key about their relationship.

If Carissa and Serenity found out about them, they literally could sabotage their plans to get away, like informing Smitty or, worse, drawing more attention to their hustle, and they could go to jail.

The plan to avoid the rest of the girls worked fine until the new holiday banquet schedule was released, and they all had to clean up after the Christmas party. Neither of them wanted to work with each other, but this time they had no choice. Black and another security guard helped as well.

At first, working together again wasn't all that bad, at least for the moment. Black and Andrea could tolerate the others enough to mask the fakeness.

It didn't last for long because as soon as Andrea stepped out to get more cleaning supplies, Carissa and Serenity started talking shit about her. Andrea had to come back because she forgot the key. She overheard Carissa kissing up to Black saying: "Andrea is just using you, and she's crazy; why can't you see that?"

Black replied, "Andrea will be back any minute; we'll talk about this later." But to Black's amazement, it was too late. Andrea barged in their conversation, immediately calling Carissa a liar. Black quickly grabbed Andrea's arm and led her to another part of the hotel to defuse a possible fight.

It wasn't a sustained attempt because Carissa relentlessly continued her hot pursuit of both Andrea and Black. Serenity followed close behind. First, they checked the smoking area in the rear of the hotel where they usually hung out, then Black's suite, but there was no luck finding them in those places either.

After thirty minutes of searching and walking around puzzled, they then decided to grab the keys from the maintenance closet to check the security cameras for their location. And it worked. Andrea and Black were both spotted heading for the laundry room; there was an office back there where they could hide. The Housekeeping and Laundry Room Managers frequently used the space for their activities.

Still, in possession of the keys, they opened the Laundry room door quietly. The manager's offices were further in the back; it was easy to sneak in undetected. It was still dark in the laundry room, and they could see there was a light on further around the corner.

They could hear heavy breathing coming from the back office as they crippled softly and slowly. Their intuitions were correct because they put their ears to the door and could listen to them inside having sex. They listened a little longer to make sure they could make their move at the precise moment.

They were not ready for what they heard on the other side of the door. Black and Andrea were close for more than one reason: they shared a common interest. Andrea was a Dominatrix at times, and Black has a secret fetish of being dominated.

Their BDSM role play allowed them to explore. The timing was perfect for them both; Black was horny, and Andrea was in one of her manias due to the frustrating lingering exchange between herself, Carissa, and Serenity.

They were supposed to remain low-key for a little longer; instead, they figured a quick make-out session wouldn't hurt. From their assumptions, no one could know they were down there. At least that's what they thought. Andrea told Black she wanted to try something she read online on a Polyandry Website.

She said, "I'm down here a lot, and I keep a paddle in my locker for my male clients that like to be submissive. Black do you like to be submissive, and will you be submissive to me," asked Andrea"? Black delightfully lit up and asked, "So let me get this straight; did you say you wanted to spank me with that paddle?" Andrea replied, "Yes, and I need you to obey all my commands while the action is taking place." Black was highly turned on and blown away; it's like she could be whatever she wanted when she wanted.

In Black's mind, he thought he would never find an attractive woman like Andrea that was into what he liked; her fetish attitude was rare and to be applauded. But he couldn't let anyone see him outside of his masculine frame, so he always kept an alpha male façade to throw off their scent.

Andrea saw right through that, made Black bend over naked, and then started whipping his ass with his own security uniform belt. She spanked Black hard, rubbed his ass softly, paused at times to stroke his penis, and kept going until she was ready to stop even though she liked to hear him beg.

CHAPTER FOUR

UNRAVELING THE MANIA

As they walked into the room, Carissa shouted, "I knew it; I knew y'all were fucking, but did he tell you that he's fucking me too? Tell her Black!" Black stood there naked and said, "Get the fuck out of here!" But the two didn't budge. Carissa added, "And he also fucked Serenity last Tuesday, so you see, you Bitch! there's nothing special about you. You're just another low-class whore for the streets just like us! Did you think you were special? Think again!"

While Carissa and Serenity were steady running their mouth as if they wanted to fight. Andrea continued to get dressed, and then it happened; they set off Andrea's first dark split. It's that moment when you're either good or bad and when things are either clear or uncertain.

Andrea covered her ears, shaking her head continually in a childlike manner, begging them just to shut up. As she turned her head to walk away, she saw a reflection in the laundry room mirror of the star of the movie The Stepfather. From that point on, Andrea wasn't Andrea. Mentally she was someone else, someone dark, someone cold.

Nearby was a sink that contained four knives in a holder on the wall. Andrea grabbed one out and sped toward Carissa and Serenity, maneuvered around Black charging Carissa and Serenity with one of the knives. They tried to step back and dodge the knife swinging, but they couldn't in time. Andrea swung and cut Carissa across her neck and, in one motion, stabbed Serenity.

After she realized they were both dead, she marked her victims with an X across their chest. Blood was everywhere. Black stood there paralyzed in disbelief, majorly shaking up. He had never seen anything like that, but unfortunately, he had no time to ponder or reflect on what he just saw because Andrea passed out, leaving him to clean up the mess by himself. The laundry room looked like a scene from a horror movie. He didn't know where to start as far as the clean-up, but he knew he had to move fast because he was caught on camera walking with Andrea hand and hand headed to the crime area. Black knew he could go down, too, if shit ever hit the fan.

Andrea awoke the following day and found herself in a rental car with Black, headed to Chicago, Illinois. They were on the run. She questioned Black as to what happened because she blacked out. Black replied, "You don't remember?" Andrea replied, "No, all I remember is an X and a lot of blood; that's it." Black told her, "Carissa and Serenity busted in while we were having sex making loud accusations. You killed them both and passed out."

Black told her he removed the murder weapon, the knife, and threw it in Lake Erie, but he lied. He put it in a safe where only he had the combination. Andrea broke down when she heard the extent of what she did.

Black never imagined she could kill two people, and worse, forget about it. She hated Carissa and Serenity. Her revenge plot was to find a ploy to embarrass them and ruin their relationship with Black; therefore, he would focus on just her.

Regardless of the intent it was too late for that because the darkness inside Andrea had grown to full fruition. This was the moment she realized the full extent of her darkness. First, she became scared because of her evilness and then the ability to commit murder and forget.

Secondly, she was scared the cops will come for her; she had watched a lot of crime shows to know he may have left something that could eventually be traced back to her. Black felt the same way, but he took comfort in the fact that he scrubbed the crime scene clean. He told Andrea how he grabbed an empty housekeeping hamper. He lined it with large trash bags and put his and her bloody clothes in it. Then he dumped the bloody linin in it and used some of the housekeeping's cleaning agents to wipe down any fingerprints, residue, or anything else that may link them to the crime scene. Last, he erased the security cameras and burned the bloody evidence, all except the knife.

Black could not hide how scared he was when they saw all the news channels were talking about what happened. He knew he had to do something, or they would forever look over their shoulders in fear of getting caught.

Once they arrived in Chicago, Black met up with his longtime friend, Tristan. He was Black's best friend growing up, so it was no surprise that Tristan was willing to assist Black and Andrea through the transition from Detroit to Chicago.

They were able to lay low and stay with him for a while. Tristan helped Andrea with a disguise and a new identity. Tristan was well-connected in Chicago and was able to get them both new IDs. When Tristan asked her, "what will your new name be"? Andrea paused and said," Simone."

"That was my grandmother's name." Black also got her a new social security number and a diary to record daily events just in case she ever passes out again. Simone was grateful and made good use of the diary. She wore the key to it as a charm on the gold necklace Monroe had given her. At the moment, these were her two prized possessions.

After several months, Simone finally removed herself from the shadows. She created a Facebook page featuring her new name Simone.

She had been off social media for some time; after changing her hair and her name, she knew she could finally get back on social media since no one would suspect she was the same person as the X murderer in Detroit.

After almost two years of lying low, Simone got bored. She lived a quiet life, working several minimum wage jobs and never staying at a place long enough to be noticed or suspected of anything. She chose odd jobs that did not attract attention.

During those two years, they kept tabs on the case in Detroit to monitor any further developments. At one point, they heard that the police found some fingerprints, but the crime scene was too contaminated to make them out. Therefore, preventing forensics from receiving a positive match. Also, there was a question as to the whereabouts of the murder weapon and a motive. The police noted that one of the knives was missing from the four-slot knife holder in the laundry room, and to this day, it hasn't shown up.

Black and Simone knew it was no time to celebrate; they were not out of the woods yet. They were the obvious suspects, and their abrupt disappearance from the hotel made them look suspicious. It's a cold case now, but behind the scenes, it's still warm.

In the third year of being thoroughly careful and invisible in every way possible, Simone finally came up with a plan to make some money and get herself back in the game.

CHAPTER FIVE

SIMONE IS BORN

She convinced Black to allow her to work as a live-in maid. She planned to stay in the homes of rich, lonely men and seduce them out of large amounts of money and gifts. The selling point to Black was that it would give them a safer way to hustle, it would distance them from the cops, and perhaps they could get a more significant score.

It would be great to find a rich man but not too rich, one that won't attract too much attention when he hooks up with the maids. And they could even operate around him, stealing stuff here and there before planning the big heist and moving on to the next with men none wiser.

Black loved the idea and immediately started posting ads for a maid-for-hire. He laid out a plan of action, time frame and delegated who does what and who gets what. But the goal came at a price. He wanted sixty percent of what Simone takes in off the top, she would get thirty, and Tristan got the remaining ten.

He told her he was the one with a plan, and he also put a house over her head, so she owed him for getting her into Chicago safely and a roof over her head. According to Black, Simone would be rotting if he had not taken extra care of the situation, she created back in Detroit.

Black knew he had Simone under his thumb forever. She did not know about his secret with the murder weapon. She still felt indebted, and oddly, he was the only person close to a family that she had; she didn't want to be alone.

Partly because Black has already seen her at her worst, she felt safe with him in her corner. No matter how tempting it was, Simone never made friends with any other person, not even Tristan. She was scared they might get too close and see her for the monster and murderer she is.

She was worried she may blackout again and probably hurt someone else. Simone stayed extra careful and stuck with Black even when he proposed a ridiculous deal that had her at a disadvantage.

While Simone did not fully agree, she had no choice but to give them an affirmative response. Soon, Tristan found the first target. His name was Nick Hamilton, a seventy-four-year-old mega-millionaire who would celebrate his seventy-fifth birthday in the coming months.

Nick had just lost one of his maids to moving, which left an opening for Simone. Nick interviewed Simone, and she was perfect to his liking. It was a slam-dunk like they had hoped because they had done their homework and prepared Simone to nail the interview with every possible answer rehearsed.

She was hired and told to start immediately. The money was decent for the next few weeks, but Black and Tristan were anxiously waiting on the big score. They had a bigger plan and spent the weeks ahead, planning and getting everyone involved up to speed. It was turning out to be even bigger than Simone hoped.

One time, she met with them and listened to them hash out their heist. They told her what they needed her to do behind the scenes. Black expressed it's time for you to step it up because the plan is dependent on your role to do what you do best.

Simone knew the pressure was on and so she went back to work. She wore skimpy maid uniforms and sweet alluring perfume; basically, there were no options off the table to get the job done. At first, it felt like nothing was working. Which kind of threw Simone off balance because she has never struggled for attention in the past.

She has always relied on her beauty and body to get the attention she wants. But with Nick, it felt like he did not notice her at all. And when he did, it was not for what she wanted. He just asked her more personal questions and seemed to care about the answers to them.

Sometimes it may be a simple "How are you?" but the warmth and sincerity in his eyes always surprised Simone. She felt a genuine family bond. A feeling she had not felt since her father went to prison. At first, she thought he was just trying to get under her skin. But after a while, she got to know that Nick liked her too, but he was more concerned about the demons she appeared to be battling.

It was apparent she had the beauty, but he couldn't help but notice Simone was disturbed. He often heard her pitching tantrums of frustration when she was alone, just like the Stepfather did in the movie. He couldn't hear everything she battled with behind him, but he listened to enough to know that there is so much mess behind her facade of superficial perfection.

He knew there was something to her no matter how much she tried to deny it at first. He was not interested in her sexually. He just wanted to help her. Using his ability to make people feel comfortable, he often pulled her to the side and consoled her. He did that from time to time, offering his assistance to her in hopes of building up trust between the two.

Not only did Nick do that, but he also recommended an image consultant, psych counseling, a fitness membership, and yoga classes. Nick also requested to pay for those services as well. Simone was very appreciative of the offer and took the kind gesture under consideration.

His offerings were a sign that the agreement between her, Black, and Tristan was working because Nick was building trust and affection with Simone. Why else would he go the extra mile to help her? But Simone felt guilty and scared.

As much as Nick was trying to help her, she could not help thinking he would run the other way when he truly realized the extent of what she was capable of. And she was also scared of what the counseling and therapy he was recommending would reveal.

While telling herself, the only reason she's doing this is that Black is making her; deep down, she felt like she did not deserve to be saved.

She did enjoy the attention from Nick. Maybe because she had some unresolved daddy issues from having her father in prison while she was young, but she loved the doting attention and care that Nick showed her.

In just months, Nick offered to promote Simone to be his assistant, which didn't mean much but because he just wanted her to be comfortable and cared for.

She even started to feel like she was living in a make-believe world where everything was perfect. But those thoughts didn't last long because Black didn't see the situation that way. He saw Nick and Simone's interactions as being counterproductive and against what they agreed upon.

Black communicated his reservations about how she was handling her relationship with Nick to Simone. She decided not to accept Nick's offerings unless they were more tangible to all of them.

At least verbally, she agreed, but deep inside, she didn't. Because Nick built a foundation of trust so strong, he ended up making Simone an ally rather than a foe.

In the meantime, Black's radar is on high alert for any possible betrayal by Simone. He could see her falling not precisely in love but getting soft when executing their plans. She was beginning to show so much affection for Nick; it did not feel fake.

For Black, he could not stop emphasizing why they had to stick to the plan; why she could not forge personal ties with Nick as they could not stay for too long. All she was supposed to do was build a good enough relationship with Nick to help them have an easy operation on the day of the specified big heist. Simone promised not to stray and assured Black that, without a doubt, she would follow through as planned.

But trying to adhere to the plan became harder and harder to comply in all actuality. Nick gave her an invitation to his upcoming birthday party planned at his estate in two weeks. Something that almost brought tears to Simone's eyes. He saw more to her than just a maid; he saw her as someone worth saving and initiating into his world.

He was going to introduce her as his assistant and even promised to link her up with some publishers at the party when she mentioned that she wanted to write a biography one day. When Nick took pictures for the local magazines and other press outlets talked to him about his coming birthday, he had Simone join him.

She did not say anything, but she was within distance if he needed anything or when he needed someone to help him get a glass of water. The major players and other city leaders would be in attendance, so it was a big deal to everyone in the town.

Tristan saw the interview on television and alerted Black. He asked Black, "Did you know he had promoted Simone from being a maid to being his assistant?"

Black responded negatively and tried to quell his anger that Simone held such vital information from him. Tristan picked up his phone and handed it over to Black. "Let's call Simone."

Black took a deep breath and took the phone Tristan had stretched to him. He dialed Simone's number and spoke to her. She explained, "that she was going to tell them later that day, but you guys beat me to it." But Black knew she was lying but tactfully didn't call her on it. Instead, he played along and devised a new plan.

He told Simone that since she was Nick's assistant now, she could access the guest list and get them into the party. Simone complied with Black's wishes and added them to Nick's event planner and guest list as her plus two, telling Nick they were her "cousins."

Nick thanked Simone for bringing them to his attention but felt something was off because she had mentioned before that she was an only child and was not close to any of her extended family. Nick typically refused unvetted guests, so allowing them to come to his home was huge. But to prove to Simone that he trusted her, he skeptically agreed to add "her cousins" to the guestlist anyway, against his best judgment.

Black and Tristan started to notice that Simone could be leaving them in the dark. They took this opportunity to see for themselves if Simone was doing her job. Their thought process was if she was not taking control of the situation, then they would. It's been months and still no results.

The only thing they've gotten from Nick thus far was given to her, which is irrelevant to what was promised. They wanted her to get sexually involved so that Nick would spoil her with gifts that they could pawn or sell off for some cash.

They also expected Nick to fall so hard for Simone and tell her about his secret stash of money and expensive art collection. Sure, the image consulting and all was good for Simone solely, but they wanted more tangible gifts. To them, the invite meant a way to access the situation for themselves.

Finally, it was the day of the party, and Simone had on a beautiful white dress bought by Nick. On the other hand, Black and Tristan showed up at the front entrance wearing jeans, t-shirts, and sport coats.

Simone greeted them at the door and let them in but confronted them, "Are you kidding me? You can't wear that in here! I told you guys to be formal, didn't I? Are you trying to mess this up for us?"

Black replied, "Chill, it's all good; we're not staying here long anyway. We'll be gone in an hour; meanwhile, Simone continued to plead with them to change, but they didn't answer her. They just shoved her to the side and proceeded into the area of the party.

They wanted to test out the situation between Simone and Nick up close for themselves, and what they saw did not look good. Simone and Nick were whispering the most, making themselves unreadable out of all the staff and guests present. And even when Simone finally introduced them to Nick, he grudgingly shook their hand. He didn't like their appearance, and his intuition told him that they must be part of the reasons why Simone was so disturbed.

Thinking they may be getting her into some sort of trouble. Nick indulged Black and Tristan anyway for Simone's sake. He introduced them to some of the other guests as well and made them feel at home.

But Nick wasn't a fool; the guest he introduced them to was also there to spy on them, just as a precaution. And his hunch was correct. It seems that one of Nick's friends overheard Black and Tristan talking to each other about Simone "becoming a problem."

They were overheard saying, "This guy is loaded, and we picked the right target." Black told Tristan, "Dude, you hit the jackpot finding this mark. Simone should be cleaning up; he looks old and gullible."

Tristan replied, "Maybe we should give her a deadline. Black agreed.

Nick pretended not to know anything and just let them leave, believing they did not arouse any suspicion. The following Monday after the party, Nick pulled Simone aside to tell her what Black and Tristan were conversing about and how she was the topic of their discussion.

Simone had to come clean and decided that the situation was getting way out of hand; she made a brave decision and told Nick the truth about their entire plan and why she came into his life in the first place.

Nick listened silently, and for a second, he didn't say anything at first, but once he digested the situation, he picked aside; he decided to stand by Simone. Simone thoroughly explained the plot against him and even told him of her percentage of the take. Nick believed her when she told him she had no intentions of following through with the plan to deceive him.

Nick ended up taking another approach instead of exiling her and firing her. Instead, he offered her assistance in case she ever needed to get away from her money-grubbing cousins' claws.

There was a genuine friendship between the two, and Nick was just what she needed to help combat her dire situation. Shortly after Nick and Simone made their peace Nick died a few weeks later, it's still speculation as to why. Fortunately for her, Nick left her a nest egg.

Nick planned with his lawyers to have money deposited into the safety deposit boxes of all his family, friends, and employees in case of an untimely death. He gave Simone a little more than the others because he felt more connected to her. The amount he left her was roughly $86,000, and she could claim it immediately without having to wait on the will reading.

When Simone got the news of the money, she was glad, but it was also bittersweet. Bittersweet because for one she will miss Nick and two: now she had to decide whether to share the cash with Black and Tristian or use the money for an opportunity for her freedom.

After pondering thoroughly over the situation, she chose to take the second option, which meant she had to outsmart Black and Tristan.

She decided to leave on the day of Nick's funeral, which was the following Saturday. She picked that day because Black gave her a deadline or a two-week grace period to come up with something big in the aftermath of Nick's death, or it was time to move on to the next target none wiser. She also got inside information from the lawyers that the reading of the will wouldn't be until that Monday, and she was sure Black and Tristan would find out about the money before then. Time was running out. In the meantime, to get Black and Tristan off her back, she used a scare tactic. Simone feed them a false rumor that Nick's death was under investigation.

Black asked, "What does that mean?" She answered, "It means the people close to Nick, like me, are all silenced by the police pending the investigation." She added, "Let me just be candid with you. Nick overheard you talking about our plot at the party, and now there are questions as to our involvement in his death."

Of course, they were all lies, but Black and Tristian had no way of knowing for sure. It bought her more time until the truth comes out that Nick died of natural causes.

The second part of her getaway plan involved her finding a way to leave Nick's burial ceremony without drawing any attention; she was going and never coming back, so she needed an excuse to leave the sanctuary abruptly. Her strategy was to fake an illness and then be excused for a moment out of the church's sanctuary.

Afterward, exit through the back door, catch an uber to Tristan's house, where her clothes are packed. She had timed it well that the guys wouldn't be home from the funeral until later. Black and Tristan ignored the Nick involvement rumors for one day and went to the funeral and burial anyway. Basically, to find out more information about the will.

But what they didn't know was Simone scheduled a uber earlier that day for her to be picked up at a specified location and time close to the church. So why they were gone, she would make her move.

She went in and grabbed her stuff already packed and hidden in the back of her closet while the uber waited for her outside. From there, she headed to the bank to withdraw her inheritance from the safety deposit box.

Once she got to the bank, it was a slam dunk. The paperwork of her inheritance from the lawyer was in hand, making the withdrawal go smoothly without a hitch. She was in and out of the bank within minutes with her money.

The last part of her escape plan was to go somewhere far from Black and Tristian's reach. She emptied her savings a week before to treat herself to a first-class flight to a new beginning. She will never forget when she made it to the O'Hare International Airport, and the ambassador looked at her ticket and said," this is a great seat! enjoy, and to have a nice flight." Hearing that was like a dream come true. To Simone, it felt like she was going from rags to riches.

The plan worked to perfection, and her escape proved to be successful. Simone took a moment of silence before boarding the plane to honor Nick and finally take a sigh of relief. Her new destination was Pontiac, Michigan, near Detroit, where she grew up.

Somewhere she knew Black would never think to look for her. Pontiac would be the last place he would think to look since it was so close to Detroit, where she was still considered a fugitive by the police. But Simone was feeling very confident in her new identity.

If she did not do anything to arouse any suspicion or draw the attention of the police, she would be fine. And if the past year proved anything, it was that people moved on fast. After everything that happened at Smitty's hotel, the place had gone bankrupt after several months of closure following an open police investigation for Carissa and Serenity's murder.

Smitty had sold the building and eventually retired. The building was torn down, and a shopping mall was built on the land. Just like that, people had moved on. She was very confident that Black would never find her, and she would also be able to start afresh in Pontiac finally.

The money that Nick left for her was enough to help her survive for up to two years, get a used car, get an apartment, and have a drama-free life. But just when she thought things would be different, the unexpected happened.

She met a nice young man that lived in the same apartment complex as she did. His name was Dallas. He introduced himself to her one day at the mailboxes in the lobby. They usually just said a few hellos, but this time Dallas shot his shot, and Simone was very receptive to his charm. He literally charmed her right out of her pants.

Dallas reminded Simone of the guys she could not date at school because she was so private and insecure. He was a 6'4 black guy with an athletic build. Simone had heard of being boy crazy, but she never had the opportunity to experience it for herself. He was a beta male type of guy that was fun to be around and surprisingly good in bed. On some dates, Dallas took her to Spencer's in the mall to get some adult novelties after hanging out at the arcade. He was adventurous like that. And it was apparent he was gitty over Simone too. The chemistry was undeniable, but Simone was still too emotionally scarred or unavailable to fully let go, which was prevalent during sex.

For example, Dallas preferred to have sex in a missionary position, constantly gripping her ass from the bottom as he thrust slow and hard. Dallas was the passionate type that likes to kiss and observe a woman's ecstasy and facial expressions as they fucked. He knew how and when to take charge; contrary to popular belief that only alpha males could do. He had an edge to him that was not overbearing but just enough to get Simone to submit sexually. Dallas would rip off her clothes and kick them aside. Simone was used to being in a power position when it came to sex, but Dallas taking charge in the bedroom came naturally to him. He would say things like, "the sweet juices of your vagina are my aphrodisiac,"; that drove Simone crazy and by her going crazy it excited him too.

As he spread her legs and put them on his shoulders, he noticed how they were delightfully shaved as he glanced at her smooth feet, which was also a turn-on for him. From that position, he kissed on and around her vagina. Dallas stiffened his tongue as hard as possible and stayed on her cliterious for 15 minutes at a time, repeating the same action over and over while rubbing her nipples and squeezing her breast at the same time.

Once he worked his way back on top of her after kissing each section of her body, she locks her arms and legs around his back tightly while he continually works the g-spot with his dick going deeper and slower. Simone wanted to reciprocate the oral, but Dallas wouldn't let her because his turn-on was being the giver, not the receiver. He would not stop until she at least reached 1 or 2 orgasm's.

The emotionally unavailable prevalence came to play when Simone would try to turn away from Dallas when he tried to kiss her, and even though he knew she enjoyed the sex, she could not allow herself to go all the way. Kissing during missionary sex was his way of gauging how high was her emotional walls.

Dallas didn't have a lot. He stayed with his brother, James, his brother's girlfriend, Olivia, their six-year-old son, and her eleven-month-old baby. It was a complicated living situation for him, but Dallas was one of those people that made everyone around him happy.

Most of his free time was spent with Simone. He would bring her lunch if she were hungry, flowers, write her poems, and help with things around the apartment.

Simone couldn't believe that there were guys out there who were sincere like he was. To her, his patience with her paid off. Proof positive after a few months, Simone was finally able to let go and kiss him for long periods of time, not looking away and looking Dallas straight in the eye. She felt free from drama and free from Black and Tristan. Simone didn't worry if they would find her or not anymore because she now had Dallas.

But sadly, it turns out Dallas was not all that he was cracked up to be while she had her secrets, Dallas also had his. His facade of happy, easy-going was used to hide his ugly, insecure side. It turns out Dallas was not all roses and a lover boy after all; he was a good guy but had trouble managing his emotions.

At times they were like vinegar and oil. While some women would think persistence is good, to Simone, it wasn't. She liked her space, and the pushing and pulling she often did drove him nuts. Meaning when her fears are triggered, she pulls away, but if given time, she would always hit him back up as if nothing happened with no justification of her whereabouts.

It was no doubt he wanted to be with her, but with a woman in her condition; she felt smothered. It was making him look obsessed. He just did not want to leave any space or opportunity for anyone else to move in on his territory.

The lack of space from Dallas would prove to be detrimental to their relationship. Of course, she gave in at times when he begged to see her, and other times she wouldn't.

Things started to get out of hand one day when Simone had to kick him out. He was having one of his episodes. It turns out he was battling his own demons like a maniac syndrome or something. She couldn't quite put her fingers on it, but whatever he was dealing with was getting on her nerves.

On that day, he had one of his many tantrums, usually over something small, especially when Simone was not giving him the attention he

NOBODY'S SUPPOSED TO BE HERE

wanted. But this time, he went too far. He came over and banged on her door loudly like she had another guy inside or doing something foul.

He was getting paranoid by Simone not answering the door, but he knew she was in there. It turns out she was just napping. He continued to bang on the door, started screaming, and drew a lot of unwanted attention from the neighbors. To try calming him down, she just let him in.

That was a bad idea because he got worse; he started throwing and breaking stuff once he was inside. He cursed and ranted and told Simone he was breaking up with her since she was not apologizing or begging him to stay. It was not the first time he pulled such a move on her; Simone knew he would be back with flowers when he was calmer, asking her to take him back and giving her a sappy excuse that it was because he loved her too much and wanted to be with her all the time.

This time, none of that was going to work. She couldn't take another minute of his antics. Normally, she kept cool-headed whenever he started his episodes, but that day, he began to trigger her. After kicking him out, a feeling came over her that resembled the incident involving Carissa and Serenity; she clutched her hands over her ears and shook her head back and forth. As he was leaving, Simone caught a glimpse of herself in the hallway mirror, and once again, the reflection was The Stepfather.

She tried to fight it, but her Borderline Evil Mania took over. At that moment, Dallas was considered her enemy, and she was ready to retaliate. She paced frantically for thirty minutes and then decided to walk over to the next building where Dallas lived to confront him.

She banged on the door with one hand and a hammer held in the other. Simone knew he was in there because he watched his brother's kids while he and his girlfriend were out or at work.

When he didn't answer, she climbed over the balcony of their first-floor apartment and began to pound out the patio doors. She yelled out, "I know you're in here, Dallas," while continuing her way through the apartment.

Dallas didn't respond, and he stayed hidden in one of the back bedrooms with his brother's kids. They locked the door and barricaded themselves inside. The kids were scared and hollering.

Dallas did what he could to help keep them calm and quiet, but it was difficult not to react when he heard Simone smashing up the living room with a hammer. Finally, after terrorizing them for so long, Simone went home.

The neighbors notified the front office of the disturbance, and the office called the police. Dallas called his brother, who was on his way home with his girlfriend, and told them what was going on. When they made it home to the apartment complex, they went straight to Simone's apartment to confront her while Dallas stayed behind with the children.

The police had not arrived yet, but James and Olivia, Dallas's brother and girlfriend banged on Simone's door to find out exactly what was up with her.

They wanted to give her a firm word not to terrorize their children whenever she and Dallas got into one of their fights. Also, they threatened her by telling her "she will pay for their property damage she did with that hammer". But nothing prepared them for what was about to happen.

All the lights had been off in her apartment, and when they knocked for the first time without any response, they assumed no one was home. But as they were about to leave, Olivia noticed the door was open; she alerted her boyfriend, but she was closer to the door, so she pushed it open and stepped inside with James behind her telling her to wait for the police.

Olivia was in mama bear mode. She was determined to have a word with the crazy lady that terrorized her children and destroyed her property. She did not know the evil mania was still in charge and had hidden behind the wall waiting quietly to pounce.

As Olivia entered the house, Simone jumped out and came out swinging two knives to their surprise. After a brief struggle, Simone killed Olivia in cold blood. She stabbed her in the belly and neck. James tried grabbing Simone from the back, but he couldn't stop Simone as she pushed him off, causing him to bang his head on the side of the bar knocking him unconscious.

Having no one to stop her, Simone proceeded to mark a bloody X with one of the knives on Olivia's chest. As she ran into her room to grab her stuff, she blacked out on the floor of her bedroom.

A few minutes later, James regained his consciousness and just stared in amazement at Olivia's dead body, similar to how Black looked after the Detroit murders. He remained sobbing for his girlfriend until the police arrived.

CHAPTER SIX

THE TRIAL AND JUSTICE

The Oakland County Sheriff Department in Pontiac swarmed the property and apprehended Simone while restraining James. He had not even known that Simone had been in the bedroom until the cops came and searched. They found her passed out on the floor, her hand and face still bloody from murdering Olivia in cold blood.

The police arrested her when she came to, and still, she seemed puzzled about what happened. After controlling a raging James and calming him down, the police let him go. But he and a few neighbors stayed and gathered near Simone's apartment in awe of what had just happened hours prior.

It was an event the neighbors will never forget. What made it so difficult was that the neighbors and the property's employees were fond of Simone and couldn't believe she could do such a thing.

First responder, Officer Ron Benet, arrived on the scene after his colleagues had come to take Simone away; he secured the crime scene, identified the witnesses, and called for the appropriate assistance. He then documented everything he saw and confirmed that it was a homicide that had taken place.

He barricaded, yellow taped the area, and used his vehicle to block the entrance. The lead detective, Sasha Cortez, came upon the scene to assist officer Benet, but when she saw who was lying there dead, she fell to her knees and cried.

She broke down because not only was she the Lead Detective on the case, but she was Olivia's aunt. Officer Benet calmed her down for the moment, just enough time to compose herself and give her the incident report. Cortez did calm down but kept insisting on seeing the suspect. The sight of her niece lying in a pool of blood made all sorts of thoughts go through her mind.

What is she going to tell the rest of the family? What's going to happen with the kids, and will Dallas and James attempt to retaliate? Those were all fair questions racing through her mind. Cortez had seen a lot of crime scenes and dead bodies, but nothing prepared her for how gory the sight of her niece would be.

Cortez had just eaten lunch with Olivia earlier that day, and she looked healthy and happy. She quickly covered her mouth when she tried to fight back a heart-wrenching sob when she saw the medical examiner examining Olivia.

Benet knew something had to be very wrong for someone who was always level-headed and professional. When he saw how Cortez reacted to the crime scene, particularly the dead body, it didn't take him long to piece together that she was related to the victim. Officer Benet pulled Cortez to the side and told her, "Detective, you are clearly in no condition to continue to work this crime scene."

He informed her that he knew she was related to the victim and that he must tell her superiors about this development. Policy states" that you cannot take on cases that proved to be too challenging emotionally to keep it together".

Nevertheless, his heart went out to her, and so he said, "If you wish to stay on until further notice, that's fine, but if not, I will keep you in the loop of the outcome.

She replied, shaking her head in disagreement, adamant about remaining on the case for as long as possible. She knew she was the best person for the job. If they took her off the case now, that wouldn't stop her anyway because she was determined to put Simone behind bars and attempt to get justice for the family.

Cortez calmed down a little and responded to Officer Benet's kind eyes and told him, "Please don't speak to the supervisors, I am fine, and I can do this. I just need a minute to breathe. Just give me a moment."

After she composed herself, she and Ron agreed she would stay on and examine the crime scene together. She tried to keep it together as they secured the murder weapon retrieved from Simone's room, collected photos, dusted for fingerprints, and took witnesses' statements; Sasha noticed a bloody X sliced across Olivia's chest. She asked herself, "Could this be a marking of some sort?" Sasha thought the X might be crucial for later follow-up, so she included it in the report.

Later that night, after pulling some strings, Cortez was finally granted a moment to speak to Simone before her lawyer arrived, but it was a waste of time. Simone would not cooperate.

She stonewalled Cortez, refusing to answer her questions while looking her straight in the eyes and ignoring her. Her attitude upset Cortez, but she continued to try to get her to talk.

Cortez got frustrated and angry when Simone requested her lawyer; that's when she slammed Simone's head on the desk in front of her. Her colleagues that had been watching closely from behind the glass quickly ran inside the interrogation room, and Cortez had to be restrained.

But she was not done with Simone. She wanted Simone to know that this was not over and that she had a new deadly enemy that would do everything to make sure she rots in prison.

This led to a shouting match between the two women. Simone screamed as her head pounded heavily after the slam on the metal table. In a way, her violence finally broke Simone's silence as she cursed at Cortez, "You're not a cop; what kind of cop does shit like this?"

Cortez shouted back, "You killed my family, bitch; I hope you burn in hell!" But she was soon taken out of there and forced to calm down. After a stern talking-to from her boss, who was disappointed by her outburst, she avoided being suspended for hurting Simone during the interrogation. When it was all said and done, Detective Sasha Cortez knew she had to face reality.

It was beyond her now. She had to leave it all up to the justice system and hope that they do the right thing and lock Simone up for good.

Simone got lucky, though. The public defender she was assigned to by the court was Isabella Romford. A bad-ass lawyer that believed in helping the helpless. The first thing she told Simone was that if she had any hope of ever seeing daylight again, she had to be open to her and be honest about everything.

Simone had heard in jail that Isabella was great and was the one person that could help her stand a chance. Isabella had the knack of taking guilty cases and turning them around, both for the media attention and because she had plans for her career. She wanted everyone to think she was a savior to people who could not afford expensive lawyers.

She took Simone's case and managed to come up with a story of a sad, mentally challenged young lady who was never treated with love and was made a sex worker when she was transitioning into adulthood. She made Simone look like the victim of a tough life who never had her mental issues diagnosed.

Cortez was working day and night to bring up new charges and finding evidence that Simone knew exactly what she was doing. Isabella kept knocking down all the charges brought up by the prosecutor. Cortez finally matched the X marking that Simone marked on Olivia's dead body to Carissa and Serenity's marking back in Detroit.

But Isabella was smart, and because Simone had been honest with her from the start, she was able to build a solid defense against that allegation too. When Simone's charges from Carissa's and Serenity's murder case came into play, those charges got dropped because there was no murder weapon.

Isabella argued that Simone had mental issues and could not be blamed for something she couldn't remember and was barely in control of. It became a long and grueling trial that finally, after thirteen months of back and forth between the defense and the prosecution, the jury came to a decision.

The jury acknowledged that she did commit a crime and killed somebody, but she was better off in a psych ward where she would get the help she needs. They believed she was mentally sick and deeply insane. The judge sentenced her to seven years in the psych ward, not prison time.

Cortez, after following the hearings judiciously, could not believe her ears when she heard the judge's verdict. She just stared in disbelief and horror at how Isabella had successfully managed to spin this case around just to salvage her reputation as a bad-ass selfless public defender.

Cortez was there with Dallas and his brother. Dallas screamed at the top of his voice, "She is not crazy! She knew what she was doing! She murdered Olivia, and you're just giving her seven years in a Psych ward. She is a murderer! Send her to jail forever! She has killed three people, and you want to let her go in seven years? This is bullshit!"

The judge had to tell the bailiff to restrain Dallas as he was screaming and kicking. The rest of Olivia's family cried because they believed that justice had not been served. But Cortez assured him they were not done with the case, and she would never stop fighting to make sure that Simone paid for what she did to their family.

During the trial, which became famous as the X Cases by the media, as more evidence was dug up about Simone's past, Terrence Black became a person of interest. Because of his role in Carissa and Serenity's murder, he was allegedly running a prostitution gang that included minors back in Smitty's hotel.

After a thorough search and with the help of Simone, who cut a deal to help them find Black, the police were able to trace Black to Chicago and arrested him.

They took Terrance Black into custody for one count of accessory to murder as they could not prove he ran a prostitution ring just because Simone said so.

Isabella had put the word out for any other girl that once worked with Terrence Black could come forward and testify against him, but no one came. He was only charged on the accessory to murder but freed from prison within three months because both he and Simone got exonerated for that crime due to the lack of a murder weapon, a murder weapon that Black still had, but he swore he did not. If he tried to expose Simone by presenting the murder weapon now, he would risk going down himself. A conviction would ruin Black's life and make him an ex-convict even after he had been trying to turn his life around after Simone ran away from Chicago with the money Nick left her.

He was so mad she dragged him down with her and painted him like he was the bad guy in her story that made her do bad things. Now both Cortez and Black were grudgingly gunning for Simone or, should I say, Andrea.

Cortez had known with Isabella on the case; it would have an outcome like this because that was what Isabella was best at doing. Over the past year, Cortez applied and eventually joined the FBI.

She had refrained from taking that route before because she was satisfied with just being a detective, but Olivia's case proved to her that the police had limited resources. If she wanted to see her niece have justice, she needed the FBI's federal authority and resources to bring Simone down.

Her transfer went through, and because she did so well, in her role as a police detective, Sasha Cortez was promoted as a Special Agent in the FBI. After the ruling that day, Isabella was hailed as a hero, and she even gave a speech to the press about fighting for the voiceless and victimizing people with mental disorders. She even started talking about the system and how she could help make it better.

Cortez was disgusted by her deception and how she tried to use the situation to progress her career. She walked up towards Isabella and stole the press's attention as they were interested in what Cortez would do next.

A reporter asked her, "Tell us, Detective Sasha Cortez, we know the person that was killed was close to you, your niece, correct? How do you feel about the verdict today? And do you think justice was served?"

Cortez responded to them, "Our whole family is distraught. Even after years of working in public service, I have never been more disappointed in my career. Losing this case is too much to bear, but in my new position and promotion to the FBI, I will have the resources at my disposal to help prevent horrific crimes like this from happening again under my watch.

Make no mistake, despite the verdict's conclusion, this woman is not crazy! She's a con artist and a killer. She will strike again, but when she does, I'll be there to take her down for good this time."

CHAPTER SEVEN

LIFE IN THE PSYCH

Simone's time at the Kalamazoo Psychiatric Hospital was eventful but needed. She underwent numerous psyche evaluations while heavily medicated. The psychological interventions and counseling proved beneficial because initially, she thought she might be bipolar for the longest time.

But in this case, the diagnosis was much different. It turns out Simone had Borderline Personality Disorder, one of the most misunderstood and stigmatized disorders. Simone accepted the diagnosis, and the Psychologist monitored her progress throughout treatment.

They taught her how to identify problems, generate potential solutions, select a solution, try it, and evaluate the outcome. But what some say helped the most was a visit from her estranged father, Monroe. The mayor of Pontiac approved a visit from Simone to the facility prison where Monroe was held.

Simone was excited but nervous about seeing her father again but agreed to the visit; so did Monroe. She had not seen him since he was taken to prison and did not even know what to say to him and their relationship. It was the time in the Psychiatric hospital that helped her realize that she had many unresolved issues.

Most of her life started to fall apart when her father went to jail; she knew it had to do with her relationship with Monroe. This time, her therapist recommended she needed to do everything she could to get better. Simone meeting with her father again after many years was one prerequisite to getting her better and managing her disorder.

She needed to know that there was somebody out there that had her back. They finally met, and after they got all their pleasantries and tears out of the way, she shared the circumstances of the conditions back in Detroit. She told Monroe what happened at the Airport Hotel after he left and how she felt when he refused to see her after his sentencing.

She briefed him on the status of her mom, Rae, Smitty, Black, and the murders she got detained for. She also told him her new name and why she was going to keep it despite of everything. She told Monroe she needed to keep it because her new identity as Simone represents the new her.

Monroe apologized for not being there and refusing her visits. He told Simone why he had to do what he had to do, and it was for their safety. Simone respectfully understood. It was time for healing, and she was just glad they were back together. He was incredibly disappointed in Rae, though, for selling off Andrea and disappearing like that; he never thought she would fold under the pressure. Thanks to Simone, Monroe finally knew the extent and repercussions of his negligence. He felt so helpless, knowing his daughter needed him and he wasn't there for her.

Monroe promised Simone he would do better as a father and use his resources, although still incarcerated, to check up on her from time to time. The mayor and the hospital really orchestrated a healthy line of communication between the two.

After that, she had several more face-to-face meetings with her dad. After continuous therapy on managing her mental condition and identifying her triggers, she was ready to be released and start a new life once again. But what they did not know was that Simone still had the hustler mindset.

She knew she had to use what she had to get what she wanted if she stood any chance of turning her life around after the years spent in the psychiatric hospital.

While she did not hope to kill anyone anymore, she still wanted to find someone to care for her. That was when she came across a magazine that highlighted me, Lonnie Guy, a New Orleans, Louisiana, rich, eligible bachelor.

CHAPTER EIGHT

OUR LOVE STORY

She saw an article in Forbes Magazine describing how I won my million's by hitting the Louisiana State Lottery and how I expanded my winnings into Billions. I was only twenty-eight years old. The magazine stated I was nominated and unanimously rated 'The Catch of the Decade' because of my looks, charm, and humility.

You would think I was superman, but I was certainly not; I had my own issues that I couldn't shake. I had a savior's complex when it relates to beautiful damsels in distress. It has become an unhealthy addiction, but that's something I was trying to work out in therapy.

I say this because I finally met a woman so broken that all the money in the world, not even a billionaire like me, could fix. If I were superman, then Simone would be my Lois Lane but with a mental disorder. Someone my superpowers could not save.

I met Simone when she responded to an ad posted in the New Orleans Times-Picayune searching for a live-in maid. Simone saw my ad and immediately tried to get in touch with me. To her, it was an answer to her prayers. The perfect job she was looking for and the perfect man.

She did her homework on the kind of person I was and hoping to make me her next target. I already looked like the perfect candidate on paper, she just needed to get close enough to me and seal the deal.

In her response to me, she included a link to her Facebook page to view her profile. Usually, I am not the one to do the hiring, but since we had many issues with the staff selling my information to the press in years prior. I decided to have a close hand in who would be selected.

When I saw her Facebook account link, I told myself I was only clicking for research, but I was curious. Her preparation worked because I viewed her profile, and I was overly impressed.

I followed her on social media for the next few weeks, and just like Nick, I was very intrigued by her. I noticed we had a lot in common such as watching suspense movies, traveling, and romance.

There have been times on Facebook I have seen her craving attention, acting desperately for likes lol, but I just ignored her antics and laughed at them. I found it quite humorous.

It was a trait that I found rare when it came down to getting to know a woman. Her fun sense of humor and her good looks sealed the deal for me. It was evident by now that I liked her.

I also liked how she was comfortable with her sexuality. I saw her go live on Facebook a few times wearing sexy dresses and high-heeled shoes. It was so refreshing for me to see a woman so comfortable with her sexuality.

Coming from the south, the women are sexy there too, but more privately and discreetly as opposed to Vegas or Miami. We even refer to our women as Southern Belles. She got my attention all right; hell, she stood out like a sore thumb.

One night, to my surprise, she inboxed me, and our interaction began. I did not say anything about the job as my live-in maid. Instead, we had some great conversations without ever seeing each other.

I tried asking about her life and her past, but I could never get anywhere. I assume the reason why was because Simone didn't want to make a wrong impression on me.

She was mysterious that way. How fitting because New Orleans is known for being a mysterious place. And to add to the mystery, she kept a key as a charm on her necklace. It was the key to her diary. Since she wouldn't tell me anything about her, I figure if I told her my story, she might open up. So, I did.

I told her growing up was tough for me as I was raised in a single-parent home, and it was even more challenging for my mother.

Simone picked up on what I meant by saying, "That's the reason why you have such a huge heart towards women and your caretaker mentality." I replied, "I assume."

I was close to my mom and the other women in my family, which Simone could tell. She said, "Well, you had to be there for your mom; that is why you're so nice."

"I saw the struggles she had to endure as a single woman raising a child alone. It was rough, especially since my father wasn't there."

The conversation was great and therapeutic, bringing us closer together. It made her see me as a person and not just a target. I couldn't wait to build on our momentum, so I asked her out on a date and waited to surprise her with the job offer at the same time.

I knew it would be tricky and that she may want to refuse the job offer, but it was no way I wasn't going to take a chance. I felt she deserved the job, but if she did not want to date me, I would not let that influence my decision to hire her.

It wasn't easy, but I tried to remain professional as possible. But there was no way I would waste an opportunity to meet this woman face to face and experience a day with her before she makes her decision.

CHAPTER NINE

FIRST DATE TO REMEMBER

Simone and I hit it off, and to be honest, she was a shoo-in for the job and hope for much more. There was no doubt she would be a great addition to my staff and potentially Mrs. Guy. But before we even got to that, she accepted my offer for a first date, so I began planning.

I spared no expense; I sent her over a gift box that included a Ralph Lauren dress, a new pair of red bottom shoes, a Birkin handbag, and money for a spa day that included a massage, hair, skin, and nails. When she received her gifts, she felt like Cinderella. Things were beginning to look up for her.

When the day came, I wanted to make one last impression on her; I had my helicopter land in a field near her house so everyone could see. She lived in a nearby city called Metairie, Louisiana, only 40 miles away.

When I finally arrived, I was amazed at how she looked; the Facebook pictures didn't do her any justice. In person, she looked even better.

Once I arrived and exchanged pleasantries, I flew Simone in my helicopter to a romantic dinner on my yacht stationed off Lake Pontchartrain near New Orleans.

The chef prepared some lamb chops for us with all the fixings and to wash it all down; we had red wine while gazing at the stars. She felt like a princess. The night was perfect, and neither of us wanted it to be over.

After dinner on the yacht, we decided to catch a late movie at the local theatre. And what do you know? The movie that was playing was her favorite childhood movie, The Stepfather digitally remastered.

You can imagine how excited she was. This was probably the best day of her life. We were the only two in the back of the theatre. That's when things started to heat up sexually. The sexual chemistry we had for each other was off the charts.

We sat in the back row like two high school kids. And about several minutes later, it was evident she was getting turned on. I could feel her heart beating fast nervously in anticipation about what was about to happen next.

So, aroused, she slightly bit her tongue but, that didn't stop her. It was that look: the way she looked at me with eyes filled with desire. She was ready to fuck, and I was too.

She must have been horny because she took my hand, raised her skirt right up to her waist, and guided my hand to her pussy. I rubbed on her clit through her panties, causing her eyes to glaze over.

I finally moved her panties to the side and slid some fingers inside her. I moved my fingers slowly in and out, deeper and deeper. I swallowed her sexy moans in an open-mouthed kiss.

After a while, she noticed my erection pressing against her thigh, so I quietly unzipped my pants and pulled out my dick. She wasted no time; she stroked the entire length of it slowly and looking me dead in my eyes. As she was stroking me, I grabbed her and whispered in her ear, "Let's do something fun." She replied, "I'm down; what do you have in mind?"

I said, "Meet me by the women's restroom door in five minutes, and you'll find out."

Right on time, she showed up walking towards me walking with that confident gait. Once she got there, she asked, what now? I told Simone to go inside and make sure that no one was in there since were about to be frolicking around in the women's bathroom. She gave me a signal waiving to me it's all clear, and then I proceeded to enter.

She locked the door behind me. This was when things took a dramatic turn. I'm not sure what came over her, but as I pulled down my pants, she pushed me back, climbed up on the cabinet, pulled up her skirt, pulled down her panties; and to my surprise, she started furiously masturbating.

That's right, masturbating and would not allow me to touch her or come nowhere near her, not even for a second. When she was done, she just pulled up her panties and walked out of the bathroom as if nothing happened.

Could you imagine my state of confusion? I was confused to the highest level.

I admit my dick was no slouch, but damn, no one has ever masturbated by just looking at it. That was a first. Thinking of being with her was as exciting as being on a rollercoaster ride with peaks and valleys, never knowing what's going to happen next. If you ask me, that's the glue or the key ingredient that makes guys like me, who were once sheltered, get obsessed.

In other words, I was hooked by her uninhibited free spirit behavior. I met her back at our seat, and it appeared that whatever kind of trance she was in was now over. Things were a little awkward between us, but nothing she did was a deal-breaker; it was just super weird.

The kind of weird that makes you want to just sit there for a second and reflect. We watched the rest of the movie, and then I took her home. On the car ride home, we never spoke about anything that took place. I walked her to her doorstep and kissed her good night. What a night! Mark this down as the first moment I can recollect that was abnormal and that she may have some sort of chemical imbalance. But still, believe it or not, I was intrigued and needed more time to try and figure her out.

This was the first of many dates; as you recall from the beginning, we had a favorite park we frequented in Metairie. We had our ups and downs, particularly about how we would navigate our relationship once she started working for me, which was why I waited a few weeks before making her officially clear to work. I knew I could not hold it in any longer; I was finally ready to take the next step and have her meet my staff and get her settled in at The Guy Estate.

CHAPTER TEN

LIFE AT THE GUY ESTATE

The following Monday, I drove her to The Guy Estate, where she would work as a live-in maid for me. When we got there, the estate was huge, and we covered the ground staff first.

I took Simone around to meet and greet everyone that worked on the grounds of The Guy Estate. We finally went inside the house, and to my surprise, when we entered the banquet hall of my estate, my whole staff awaited to welcome her.

If truth be told, it was not like them to extend such warm hospitality. The staffers were not fakers, especially my female staff; they knew I thrived on honesty and loyalty, so if they did not like someone, I knew they would not put on a show for my sake.

I was surprised my female staff extended their hospitality so wholeheartedly. They were usually skeptical of anyone new that I dated or worked for me. I assumed this is because I spoke so highly of

Simone, and they saw how happy I had been recently since I started dating her.

I honestly didn't know what to expect, but I'm glad they embraced her. It turns out she had mutual respect for them too. But when I showed her to her room as we toured the rest of the house, I learned that Simone had her reservations.

She read about my live-in maids and me in a recent Forbes Magazine article, where the Forbes team questioned my love for the beautiful women that make up my well-paid staff. And when Simone brought it up, I just chuckled and said, "About that…"

"They made me out to be Hugh Hefner or someone of that nature, but it was just a coincidence they look like that; that wasn't my intention at all. But don't worry, honey, you have nothing to worry about; my love for them is strictly professional. Besides, I'm always too busy being wrapped up into their baggage to form a connection with them." Let me explain.

First, there was Melania, a super sexy Columbian and the comedian of the group. She had this funny country ascent and would say random crazy stuff that would get everyone laughing. We loved her personality. Her issue was she always kept going back to assholes who abused her.

The next was Tina, the elder and leader of the group. She was forty-two years old but still looked amazingly attractive. She kept herself in great shape, and her skin was flawless. Her son's friends even try to hit on her and even labeled her the 'MILF of the Decade.'

Back in her younger days, she won several pageants and did a famous magazine spread. Her psychologist says she has a histrionic personality disorder, which is attention-seeking behavior. For example, she is the drama queen type who is always in my ear for every little thing.

Next, there was Pamela. Pamela is a cute six-foot-one bombshell from up north. We call her Pam, and she was the newest and the youngest of the maids in the group. She came two months before Simone.

Pam just wanted to fit in with the others and me. She was also the loner, an introvert who mostly hung out with the men on the estate. Pam's baggage consists of being a recovering drug addict but has been clean for two years. I agreed with her that if she stays clean and keeps going to her meetings, I will allow her to continue working on my estate for as long as she wants.

Simone was happy that even though I still had a savior's complex towards women with baggage, I did not get involved with them. I was just adamant when it came to looking out for them. And that she was the exception.

Simone's relationship with the other maids started out good but became rocky quickly. The ladies were not accepting of Simone's background story of her being an orphan that grew up in the middle of nowhere.

But if her identity or past gets out, it could be detrimental to her plans to marry me. For instance, when I sent Simone, Tina, and Melania to the neighboring city, Baton Rouge, to pick up the new staff uniforms.

During the ride over, Simone got a disturbing phone call from an anonymous caller. He said, "I know where you are, and I'm coming to get my money."

Then the call ended. Seeing how visibly shaken Simone got, Tina and Pam asked her in a very concerned way,

"Who was that on the phone, Simone?" Tina asked.

Simone replied, "It has to be a prank, never mind."

The ladies dismissed it as that could have been true. While they were chatting about the phone call, the phone rang again. This time, with Simone's permission, Tina answered the phone and asked, "Who is this? What do you want?" This time the guy on the other line replied, "She's not who she says she is; ask her what her real name is?" Simone could hear what he was saying, causing her to go into an outrage, so she grabbed the phone back from Tina and ended the call. She told the others, "It's not true, and I do not want to hear another word about this."

The whole situation left both Simone and the others puzzled. The anonymous calls led to more questions than answers, and Simone needed to make sure the incident stayed between them. The girls asked Simone, "Are you sure you don't want us to involve Lonnie?" Simone replied, "Please don't. I'll figure this out; no need to get him involved when we don't have to."

These phone calls were like deja vu to Simone. It was like watching The Stepfather movie all over again, but she was the one starring in this movie. Any more of those close calls or red flags could ruin her plans. But just when she thought it couldn't get any worse, it did.

A few months later, when everything seemingly was back to normal, Simone was pulled over by the police for speeding. She was going fifty-five miles per hour in a forty-mile per hour speed zone. When the officer approached the vehicle, they asked her for her driver's license and registration.

She began to shuffle through her purse to get the identification when several IDs fell out. Big mistake, because Tina and Pam noticed, which made Simone look even more suspect. They bombarded Simone with questions, and they wanted answers. Especially Tina.

She threatened to report the incident to the boss immediately, which caused Simone to blow up horribly. Like the Stepfather, once her identity was threatened to come out then all gloves were off causing her to retaliate.

When they got back to the estate, Tina went frantically looking for me. She didn't get too far because before you knew it, Simone grabbed Tina and pushed her to the ground, yelling and screaming.

She yelled out, "If you tell Lonnie anything, that's the last thing you will ever do. The lawn staff rushed over to break them up, and that's when Simone knew she might have just messed up even more.

Simone remained sitting down, huffing and puffing while Tina walked off, mumbling. It was clear Simone knew it was a matter of time before Tina told me everything.

CHAPTER ELEVEN

WHAT HAPPENED TO TINA?

The next morning Tina was found dead in a pool of blood at my estate. Tina appeared to be stabbed on her right side, and her back marked with a bloody X. The groundskeeper, Hector, found her dead by the pool and called 911.

Before long, the whole staff was outside, including me, to witness this chaotic scene. While everyone stood there in tears, the New Orleans PD made it onto the property. They questioned all my maids, me, and of course, Simone.

She was the prime suspect because of the argument she had with Tina on the previous day, which meant she had a motive. Not only were the police on the scene, but reporters swarmed the property too. At this point, the whole place was in an uproar.

The police tried shielding off a few of the reporters, but they somehow snuck in anyway. I was furious. I begged and pleaded with the police and the reporters to give me a minute to digest what just happened.

We were trying to make heads from tails of this situation. Each maid and staff were interviewed one by one, not knowing what the other said during questioning. The X marked on the victim's body caught the officer's attention.

The fact that there was a distinct marking on the body prompted the authorities to notify the FBI. The marking took the interest of the newly appointed FBI Agent Sasha Cortez, the then detective in Michigan who suffered the loss of her niece due to Simone's hands. When the case got to her attention, she had to step away for a moment and gather herself.

She smiled and thought to herself, could this be her, and in New Orleans? Sasha immediately coordinated with the FBI Headquarters in New Orleans and started her investigation. This time with all the government resources at her disposal.

Meanwhile, my staff and I grieved greatly over the death of Tina. Simone mourned along with us despite the rumors. When the smoke cleared a few days later, Simone saw Lonnie was overwhelmed and could use a getaway.

A getaway couldn't have come at a better time. She took the initiative and demanded that I let everyone take a few weeks off to gather themselves while we did the same. I agreed; I let the staff off and packed my bags for a brief getaway.

NOBODY'S SUPPOSED TO BE HERE

Simone took me on a plane to Southwest Louisiana, Lake Charles, with her own money. We stayed at the Chateau Charles Hotel. We did a little gambling on the riverboats and took a long romantic walk by the Lake Charles Civic Center boardwalk.

After a fun day of holding hands and romance, we went back to the hotel room. Without a moment's hesitation, Simone pushed me against the wall, unzipped my pants, and began to give me oral sex right then and there.

This time I tried pushing her away as I was still dealing with the loss of one of my staff members who was killed. The last thing on my mind was sex, not to mention my skepticism of her possible involvement in Tina's death.

I repeatedly told Simone to stop, but it's no stopping her when she's in one of her manias. It was like trying to wake up a sleepwalker, and you know you're not supposed to do that. She even took our erotic sexual encounter to another level by opening the hotel room blinds while we fucked against the window.

Despite my skepticism, the sex was hot— scorching! We could see the people staring and pointing at us from across the way at the Doubletree hotel. I noticed the sun was starting to set, and darkness was creeping up upon us, but it was no doubt you could still see us vividly. The residents who were watching us across the way were turned on too, I suppose, considering they couldn't stop watching.

My view was different; what I saw as I stood behind her while the blood circulated from my head down to my dick, filling my nine inches to full capacity, was a goddess with supple breast and soft skin, wearing nothing but my favorite fragrance by Christian Dior; getting sexually pulverized harder than she has ever gotten pulverized before.

Cliché was not the word to describe the following sequence of events for Simone, and I hit a first on so many levels.

It's not every day you see a billionaire utterly naked for the world to see, oblivious to who was watching; and not concerned about the tabloids.

At one point, I had to take a moment to gather myself as her pussy was getting tighter and tighter. I tried to fight the feeling, but Simone wouldn't allow me to. I could feel my dick throbbing so much until I took it out for a second, but she just put it right back inside her. However, this time she squirted all over the window, not once but twice. Simone had never squirted before, yet we continued for 45 minutes more until I finally came too.

Still, in ecstasy, I turned her around towards me for a kiss, and I noticed she was crying. I asked Simone, "are you crying"? She attempted to answer but midway through her reply; she passed out. I didn't know what to do, so I hurried up, closed the curtain, and dialed 911. I'm glad everything was okay with her; the paramedics cleared her and advised me to let her sleep for a while.

While she rested, I referred to a book I had on Borderline Personality Disorders, and as I suspected, her tendencies fell in line with what I read. The book explained her risky sexual acts and mood fluctuations as well. But I had to be careful with my diagnosis because I didn't know how she would react if I told her. Plus, I'm not a hundred percent sure if that's what she has.

On the way home, Simone and I had a heart-to-heart talk. I had to address the elephant in the room. I asked her, "Simone, I have to know, and I was hoping you could tell me the truth. Did you have anything to do with Tina's death?"

She answered immediately without a moment's hesitation, "No," and I believed her. I also asked her, "What about the anonymous phone calls and threats you've been receiving? Do you think those people have anything to do with her death?"

She said, "I don't know, I hope not; I'm still trying to figure out who it could be." Again, I believed her, but I had one last question. "Is there anything I need to know about your past? Like what you're keeping in your diary?" She said, "No, I don't have anything to tell, but one day I will share what's in my diary because I would like to let go of my past and be completely open to you." I responded, "I hope so because I'm falling for you and those blackouts are concerning.

It was great that Simone and I declared our love, cleared up some gray areas, but we were not close to being out of the woods yet. When Simone got back to her room, she noticed her diary was missing. She checked the side pocket of one of her luggage bags, and just like she thought, it was missing. It was clear that someone had taken it.

She frantically had to find who may have it. The diary contained sensitive information about her time at the Psychiatric Facility, event accounts during her blackouts, the cons pulled with Black, and her murderous past.

She knew if the diary gets into the wrong hands, it will expose her, and it would prove that she's capable of killing Tina.

Simone knew she had to act quickly to recover what was missing, but the first thing she needed to do was to attempt to reach me on my cell phone to assist in her search.

When I didn't answer, she panicked. She tried calling several times more, but there was still no answer.

Her anxiety began to set in because now both I and the diary were missing. While running frantically through estate hallways, Simone came across Melania and begged for her assistance.

Melania wanted to help, but she couldn't because she was already running late for a previous engagement. But just when Simone wanted to give up, she got a brilliant thought. If she could find my iPad, then she could use the locator to track my apple watch.

The iPad proved beneficial because Simone located a signal in my neighboring pool house. She didn't want to go by herself, so she attempted to get Hector, the groundskeeper, to chaperon her, but that ended up being a waste of time. It was a waste of time because he picked today out of all days to want to flirt.

She told him, "I'm sorry I can't because I'm involved with Lonnie." Hector apologized for his terrible timing and inappropriate behavior and stormed off, telling her, "I didn't know, I'm so embarrassed."

It was clear she would have to continue the search for me alone. And time was running out. Her head was spinning because she thought about those threatening phone calls from the other day. She was sure that several people might be after her, and then they may want to hurt me to get to her.

Simone prepared for the worst. The first thing she did was double back to get a gun from her closet. A nine-millimeter she bought around the time she was receiving those anonymous calls and threats. She proceeded to the pool house. She held the iPad in one hand and the gun in the other.

Her goal was to get as close to me as she could without being detected. She tried peeping through the window, but she was unable to see anything.

She noticed the door was slightly ajar, proceeded in. With the gun in hand and iPad in the other, she yelled out, "Lonnie! Lonnie!" but there was no answer.

When Simone hit the light switch, she got blindsided. Someone used an expert karate skill to kick the gun out of her hand and hit her on the head with a pistol grip. The impact made her pass out.

When she regained her consciousness from the hit, she couldn't see anything. Everything was still a blur. She tried moving her hands, but they were handcuffed to a workout machine. When she fully regained her focus, she could see two people were standing there. At first, she had trouble making them out, but when she did, to her surprise, it was Black and one of my maids, Pamela.

CHAPTER TWELVE

LONNIE!?

Yes, Black was back and with a vengeance! Black asked Simone, "Are you surprised to see me? I don't know how you got away knowing what you did, but today is the day of redemption and my payday. Lonnie knows all about you, and by the way, here's your diary."

Simone replied, "so you're the one who made those threatening phone calls. Wow, really Black?! That was a dumb move, if you ask me," Black replied, "Yes, that was me, and I don't care if you thought it was dumb.

It achieved what I wanted it to. Now because of your stupidity in thinking that you were safe here in this secluded mansion of a billionaire, your man, Lonnie, will have to catch the brunt of your discretions. He's completing a wire transfer to us for two million dollars from his bank to ours as we speak.

Once it's done, we'll leave you two love birds alone to discuss what he knows about you. That is my type of revenge for you because you ran away and left me stranded in Chicago; and for dragging me down with you when you went to jail."

Simone replied, "No, Black, please, I'll get you the money; please leave him out of this. Pamela, and you of all people? You disloyal bitch, how could you do this to me and especially Lonnie? He accepted you and loved you despite of all your baggage, and this is how you will repay him."

She cursed at Pamela, who managed to keep a straight emotionless face throughout. When she saw that she could not get through to Pamela, she faced Black again and tried to reason with him, "Black, Nick told me not to trust you. So, I did what I had to do. I am truly sorry, you had to pay for my crimes, but that was out of my hands."

"You dumb ass slut! Your for the streets! It was never out of your hands. You knew exactly what you were doing. When Nick died, you could have given me and Tristan a cut of the money, and we would go our separate ways, but you chose to run away. You made me an accessory to a crime when all I did was help you clean up and escape without being arrested.

Instead, you went ahead and killed another person and dragged me down while I was already trying to rebuild my life. You're lucky we got acquitted because it would'nt be a conversation if we didn't; you would be dead already. I put myself on the line for you and helped you start over? You fucking disloyal cunt!"

Simone and Black's exchange sparked a response from me. Black had ordered me not to say a word until the transaction was complete, but I could not hold it in any longer. I finally broke my silence and yelled out, "Simone, just who the hell are you?" Simone's eyes bulged as she saw that I was there listening all along and must have heard the things they said to each other.

I went on, "Look at what you've done. You could have told me about your life, now look at what's happened?"

Simone replied with tears in her eyes. Afraid she had lost me forever as I was starting to know the truth about her past, "I was going to tell you everything, Lonnie.

I was just too scared. I was scared that you would leave me and never want anything to do with me when I told you about my past and everything I have done. I didn't want to lose you. Black is a part of my past that I was trying to forget, and as for Pamela, I had no idea she was in on this entire operation."

"Shut up, just shut up!! Both of you," Pamela ordered. She was finally choosing to speak. Pamela waving Simone's gun at me, ordered me to finish the wire transfer at gunpoint.

Meanwhile, Black and Simone went back and forth in their heated verbal exchange. They had a lot of unfinished business. Simone wanted answers, and Black indulged her. He braggingly told her of his exploits by breaking down what led him to her step by step.

He started narrating an account of his heist, "You always knew I was good at planning heists and cons, but I bet you didn't know that I was also good at planning more, huh? I would bet you didn't know when I got acquitted of your murders of Carissa and Serenity; I started monitoring your whereabouts. I met Pamela in Chicago, and we became partners.

She's in it for the money; I myself want the money and the perfect revenge for what you did to me. I had Pamela move wherever you moved so the setup could be complete. From there, everything went perfectly; Pamela killed your co-worker Tina, making her a copycat killer. The plan worked perfectly because all the fingers pointed at you.

We knew all we had to do was piggyback off the fight you had with Tina and make sure to mark the body with an X to incriminate you. That would be the perfect link to your previous three murders. This time, with a motive, you cannot plead mental issues or insanity. It would be clear you had a reason to kill Tina even while you were thinking clearly.

Simone replied, "Well, I have to admit you got me Black, but what does this have to do with Lonnie? Please leave him out of this."

Black replied, "Yeah, you're right. I don't want to be the one to punish another innocent person that you managed to drag into your mess. I know firsthand how that feels.

I would bet you had that poor man fall in love with you. Classic Andrea. I am not even surprised he fell for it. But it's up to you guys to resolve. After the transfer is complete, I'll let him go but not a second before then.

Simone shouted out, "No! This is not like that. Lonnie don't give them shit! I'm sure someone is looking for us by now."

Black laughed off her threats and told her no one was coming, and he could even change his mind and kill me in front of her now that he knows she has feelings for me. He told her it would be an act of perfect revenge.

Simone screamed in rage, "If you hurt him, trust and believe me, Black, I will kill you! I will kill you with my bare hands." Simone fractured her wrist to free herself from the handcuffs in an attempt to defend me when Black started to point the gun at me.

Simone then jumped onto Black's back, shouting, "Don't! I love him," but it was too late for her to fight for my life.

She was outnumbered. Pam calmly pulled out Simone's gun she had confiscated earlier and shot at Simone, a close-range shot to her back. It was a potentially fatal shot that could have damaged her organs or killed her immediately, but Pam did not care.

Black shouted out, Pam, "What the fuck did you do?! We were only supposed to get the money, you idiot! Not kill anyone! You're stupid!" Pamela then pointed the gun at Black, and before he could even react, she shot him too. This time, a deadly close-range shot to his head. She shot Black because she knew he knew too much and could give her up to the cops when push came to shove, and she could not risk it.

Fortunately, Simone didn't die; she survived but was in critical condition. Black, on the other hand, didn't make it. He took another shot to the chest near the heart, which killed him instantly. Pam confirmed the money transfer had gone through and got away.

Lucky for her, she made it out in time because just fifteen minutes prior, a neighbor heard gunshots and called 911.

Soon after, the authorities came swarming the property again. The neighbor who called the police met them at the estate gate and informed them where they heard the gunshots. They pointed to the pool house.

Once the paramedics and police located the victims, they rushed Simone to the hospital and pronounced Black dead on the scene. It was a miracle Simone survived.

The bullet did not hit any vital arteries, but she went into a coma. While unconscious and in a vegetative state in the hospital, I remained there with her despite the deception and lies she unveiled.

Now wasn't the time to deal with that or our future together; she needed someone by her side. I just knew I didn't want to lose her, so I hung in there with her through the two surgeries. I wasn't supposed to be there, but I was because I love her.

She had to have two surgeries. One was to remove several bullet fragments from her lungs, and the other was to stop the internal bleeding. While Simone was in surgery, the remaining estate staff stood by waiting for an update and an explanation of what happened at the pool house. I explained to them that I couldn't say much about what happened to Simone or the events that took place at the pool house because we're still in the middle of an investigation.

As the weeks went by, I finally got briefed by Simone's doctor on her condition. The doctors informed me that the surgery went well, but there could be complications going forward because of the trauma she experienced and her mental condition. I replied, "What kind of complications?" He answered, "It may be months before she fully regains her memory again."

Meanwhile, the police, the media, and the FBI were frantically trying to piece together what happened. Once it all came together, some were not satisfied with the outcome, including FBI Agent Sasha Cortez. She had to accept that her date with revenge has been delayed once again because Simone didn't kill Tina. But I got a feeling their day will come eventually.

As for Simone, she's getting better, but it could be months before she regains any memory or be back to normal, but she is awake and responding.

She recently remembered a memory that involved Smitty hovering over her body, having his way with her sexually with Rae's blessing. She remembered so vividly his bloody X tattoo tattooed on his neck and him dripping sweat all over her. It's no wonder she marked her victims with an X. History tells us that X tattoos are generally associated with something wrong. Her doctors also said I should be expecting random flashbacks or nightmares like this one to happen often.

I realized I had an unexplainable unconditional love for Simone. Since she was willing to risk her life to save me, at this point, I don't care what people think or say; I will always stick by her side. I definitely lost myself within all the chaos surrounding her therefore it was only one more thing left to do. To satisfy my curiosity and take a look in the box in her storage unit labeled "my life". The first time I saw the box was a few days ago when I fetched a few clothes for her during her time in the hospital. I told myself I wasn't going to invade her privacy, but I knew if I didn't take the chance now, I may never get this opportunity again. There I saw the plethora of information I spoke about at the start of the story. It included the untold story that the diary left out. After I read it completely, I realized it was no more mystery to solve and after I was done reading, I made a conscious decision to be there for her always and never to bring up her past or what happened again.

When Simone was released from the hospital to me three months later, I proposed to her live on television for the world to see and Simone said "yes". It appears that her rags to riches fairy tale is going to come true after all. She got her memory back and defied all the elements standing her way; and she's become spiritual. She prays for peace, love, and happiness and so far, things are on the right track. It appears that Simone finally beat the odds and will be planning a wedding to be the wife of a of billionaire.

In the days to come security alerted me that someone was at the estate gate demanding to get in. He identified himself as Monroe Lockett, Simone's father. Simone had no idea he was here, or he was coming.

I read about him in Simone's biography. I learned enough about him to know he's no one to play with.

Monroe's parole hearing went well, and he was released on good behavior. He wasn't supposed to leave the state of Michigan as part of his conditions, but he needed to see his daughter. He heard about what happened to her and the wedding proposal on television that's how he knew where to find her. After I verified his identity, my curiosity got the best of me, so I let him in.

When I opened the door, there stood this tall well-dressed man with a scar below his eye and a cigar in his mouth that looked scary. He asked if he could see his daughter? And said I said yes of course and I showed him the way to her. When he got to Simone's room, he requested to be alone with her. I granted his wish. Simone was under deep medication and was asleep at the time.

Monroe looked down at his Simone as she slept and gave her a kiss on her forehead. Simone opened her eyes and smiled. It was like she could sense his presents. She was glad to see Monroe and for the first time in years she finally felt at peace. She asked" how did you get out so soon"? and how did you know where to find me? He replied, I'm on parole and I heard about what happened to you and your where abouts on television. Monroe then had a question of his own. Is this guy Lonnie treating you right? She answered, "yes he's wonderful, just the type of man I wanted but, never knew I needed. I love him". Omg I just thought about something, now that you're out, can you walk me down the aisle? Monroe replied, it would me my honor.

Everything was perfect but unfortunately, in her Borderline condition she was always waiting for the other shoe to drop. And in this instance, she was right to think that because it was about to. Evil was lurking in the background and her name was Agent Sasha Cortez who still vows revenge. Sasha was no longer the by the book, squeaky clean FBI agent anymore. She made it a point to not be because after Simone slipped through her grasps the last time, she threw all of the rules out of the window.

Sasha summoned up some male family members to join her on her conquest to kill Simone on the day of her wedding. The wedding was in two weeks and she her posse in place ready to execute Sasha's plan to kill Simone.

Little did Simone know that she was in for a new battle but this time she was not alone; Monroe has her back and I do too!